"There is no 'this.'"

Corrine said it with a finality she didn't feel.

Mike ran a finger over her jaw, down her throat to the base of her neck, where her pulse had taken off. "Liar," he chided softly as her nipples beaded and thrust against the material of her shirt.

"There *can't* be a this," she whispered.

"Oh, there's definitely a this." His finger continued its path over her collarbone to her shoulder, nudging the edge of her tank top off it. Stepping even closer, he dipped his head and nipped at the skin he'd exposed, while his fingers continued their seductive assault on her senses.

"How can you ignore me?" He dipped his head so that she could feel his breath on her skin. "After what we shared?"

"It was…just…sex," she panted as he dragged that clever mouth back up her throat now, feasting as he went, his fingers toying with the edging of her top and the curve of her breast.

"Yeah. Sex. *Great* sex."

Dear Reader,

I love reading THE WRONG BED books within Temptation. Writing them is a dream come true, and so was *Her Perfect Stranger*, a book that haunted me from day one until I finished.

Ever done something you regret? Commander Corrine Atkinson, the heroine in this story, does when she succumbs to a sexy, gorgeous stranger rather than face a stormy night alone. Yet the most incredible, erotic night of her life turns into a nightmare when she's introduced to her new copilot...the very stranger she'd been with only the night before.

I've pitted two confident, dynamic, strong-willed (read: stubborn) people together, both of whom think their life is too full for love. They both learn how wrong they are. How lonely they are.

And how easy it is to fall hard in crazy love in spite of themselves.

Happy reading,

Jill Shalvis

Books by Jill Shalvis

HER PERFECT STRANGER
Jill Shalvis

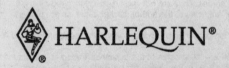

HARLEQUIN®

TORONTO • NEW YORK • LONDON
AMSTERDAM • PARIS • SYDNEY • HAMBURG
STOCKHOLM • ATHENS • TOKYO • MILAN • MADRID
PRAGUE • WARSAW • BUDAPEST • AUCKLAND

To Bruce and Leslie,
for all your expertise, patience and,
most of all, friendship. Without you,
this book wouldn't have happened. Thank you.

ISBN 0-373-25978-6

HER PERFECT STRANGER

Copyright © 2002 by Jill Shalvis.

1

HE'D NEVER FORGET his first glimpse of her. Or his second. She walked in as if she owned the place, and in spite of the chaos around him, Mike Wright's gaze went straight to her.

It was all indelibly imprinted on his mind: the harsh storm outside pounding against the fogged windows of the hotel's pub; the lights flickering overhead as the electricity spiked with the repeated thunder and lightning; the loud strains of Bruce Springsteen blaring from the speakers mounted on the walls; and the even louder voices of the crowd around him talking, laughing, flirting.

He'd been preoccupied, thinking about the reason he was in Huntsville, Alabama, in the first place—his life's work, flying space-shuttle missions. The primary pilot of STS-124 had broken his leg parachuting and the first team backup had contacted hepatitis. All of which left Mike, once the secondary backup, as primary. He'd been called home from Russia, where he'd been on loan from NASA to the Russian space agency for the past decade.

Mike loved being an astronaut, loved his testosterone-run life. But he loved women, too. All of them, all shapes and sizes and colors and temperaments, and everything else faded away the moment she stepped foot into the place—the storm, the crowd, the noise, everything.

She was wet. Drenched, actually, her dark, dark hair plastered to her head, her clothes molded to her body.

Another poor, unsuspecting victim of Huntsville's weather.

He could empathize, having just come from Russia's much more predictable climate. But this woman didn't look like anyone's poor, unsuspecting victim, not with all that attitude, fire and rage spitting from her eyes.

Drenched *and* inconvenienced, Mike guessed. And furious because of it. Amused, he watched as she pressed on through the thick crowd, and in spite of her petite stature, people moved out of her way.

It might have been the fact she was a woman,

when most of the patrons were men. On-the-prowl men at that. But Mike thought it was most likely her queen-to-peasant look, which was icily effective.

She worked her way closer, heading directly toward the bar, and by coincidence, him.

"Something hot," she demanded of the bartender, setting one hand down on the bar as she dropped her bag, establishing a spot for herself where there was none to be had. She looked to both sides, left then right, clearly expecting someone to get off a stool so she could sit.

Grinning now, Mike rose. "Please," he said, gesturing for her to take over his seat.

"Thank you." As if she wasn't dripping a river of sleet and rain onto the floor, she sat and tossed back her hair. When the bartender slid what looked like an Irish coffee in her direction, she nodded her head regally and sipped. And then sighed. Sinfully. Her shoulders relaxed slightly, as if she'd just dropped the weight of the world.

After a good long moment she appeared to realize Mike was still standing next to her. Her dark-blue eyes were cool and assessing, in direct contrast to her wet, incredibly lush, incredibly sexy body.

"No coat?" he asked, referring to the fact that she wore only a black, long-sleeved silky blouse and skirt, both of which were so wet they couldn't have been tighter if she'd painted them on. What should have been a very conservative, businesslike outfit became outrageously erotic, especially given that she had a body that could make a grown man drop to his knees and beg.

"Someone stole it at the airport." She grimaced. "I hate airports. Let's just say this is a day better forgotten all around."

She didn't have the Southern drawl of the people around him. Another misplaced traveler, he thought, just like him. "Got caught by surprise in the storm, did you?"

"Yes, and I hate surprises."

Her voice was as cool as her eyes. Low and slightly husky. But combined with all those feminine curves, she became one irresistible contradiction. Fire and ice. Tough, yet sexy as hell.

Though Mike had planned to have only one beer, which he'd already had, before going up to his room and crashing for the night in preparation of the crazy week ahead, he didn't budge. And when the guy behind him vacated his barstool, Mike took it for himself.

"Don't bother," the woman said without even looking at him as she continued to sip her drink, staring directly ahead.

Mike made himself comfortable, which included smiling at the pretty female bartender. "Don't bother what?"

"Trying to charm me out of my panties."

Mike laughed. This woman was truly sexy as hell, gorgeous as sin, cool and regal, *and* funny. A rarity. "Now why would I try do to that?" he asked innocently, though now that she'd planted the thought, he could think of nothing else.

"Why? Hmm. Maybe because I have breasts? I don't know." She shrugged. "It's a male genetic disorder, I guess."

Mike laughed. "You mean I can't help myself? That's a handy excuse, indeed."

She looked at him then, a hint of a smile on her lips. "That's right. As a man, you can't help yourself, you're just a helpless slave to your body's cravings. Will that help you sleep at night?"

"Oh, yes. Thank you." Mike cocked his head and studied her. She was warming up, no doubt thanks to her drink. There was a blush to her cheeks now, and when she crossed her legs—remarkably well-toned legs, he couldn't help but notice—they appeared to be drying nicely.

"To be quite honest," he said. "I hadn't entertained the notion of charming you out of your panties at all."

She slanted him a doubtful glance.

"Really." He lifted his hands in an innocent gesture. "Before you came, I was just going up to bed."

"Don't let me stop you."

But she did. Everything about her stopped him cold, and it wasn't just that her nipples were pressing against the material of her blouse, or that her skirt clung to her perfectly rounded hips. It wasn't just that she smelled like heaven and sin all in one, or that he knew instinctively that her skin would be soft and creamy and in need of being warmed up by his hands and mouth. He couldn't name exactly what kept him there watching her, why she fascinated him so.

Everything in his home country fascinated him, and he enjoyed being back after so long away, even given the work ahead of him. He needed lengthy training for the upcoming mission, training that would keep him busy day and night until launch, only four months off now.

He'd be far from his own place, which happened to be a suitcase more often than not these days. In fact, he was no longer certain where home really was. He and his four brothers were close, but they were also scattered across the globe, in various military branches. So was his father.

His mother, a native Russian, had died when Mike—named Mikhail by her—was very young, which was probably why, when he'd had the chance to go to Russia after his stint in the Air Force, he'd jumped at it, wanting to understand the heritage he'd missed. He'd welcomed the opportunity to stay there, in the cosmonaut space program, working on the International Space Station. It was a lifestyle he loved, but he suddenly realized how isolated from female companionship he'd been lately.

A sharp bolt of lightning startled the large, noisy bar into an instant of collective silence. Thunder rolled immediately on its tail, and after another instant of stunned quiet, the room went back to its dull roar.

The woman next to him pushed her drink away and sighed. She shivered once, then crossed her arms. "Well. Back to work."

Yeah, he should be working, too. He had

plenty of reading to do. From now until launch, he'd be living and sleeping this mission, running like crazy to catch up with his crew—whom he'd not yet met—and who'd been training together for a year and a half already. He looked forward to meeting everyone involved, but at the moment, as the woman next to him shivered again, work and everything that went with it were far from his mind. "You have business at this hour?" he asked, slipping out of his jacket and putting it around her shoulders. "What do you do?"

Those midnight-blue eyes shot his hands a sharp glance, causing him to lift them from her shoulders. "I have some reading to catch up on," she said, snuggling deeper into his jacket. "Thanks for the coat."

"Reading?"

"I don't really care to discuss it."

"Touchy about work," he said with an agreeable nod. "Duly noted."

"Good."

"How about your name? Are you touchy about that, too?"

Reaching once more for her drink, she tossed her head back as she downed the last of it, then licked her lips in an uncalculated, outrageously sexy move that made Mike want to groan. "Tonight," she eventually said, her full, bottom lip wet now from her own tongue, "I'm touchy about everything." But she made no move to get up. "I don't want to talk about my job, my name, my life. I don't want to talk about politics or headlines." She lifted those amazing eyes to his. "Still want to have a conversation with me or have I scared you off yet?"

There was more than a little dare in her expression, and Mike, the youngest of four boys in a military family, had never, not once in his life, walked away from a dare.

Lightning struck just then, and when the thunder came right on its heels, everyone in the room oohed and aahed.

Not the woman sitting next to him, though. Her gaze remained intense and direct and right on his, so that he hardly noticed the ruckus going on outside. He did, however, notice the growing crowd, as more people made their way in from the storm. Which was fine by him, as it forced him slightly closer to the woman still waiting for his answer.

"I don't scare easily," he eventually said.

"I'm losing my touch then."

"Tell me your name."

"Why?"

"I feel the need to call you something."

"Fine. Call me Lola." She lifted a brow in what might have been either self-deprecation or wry humor. "Yes, tonight Lola will do."

Oh, definitely, she was warming up. Her skin was glowing and rosy. And her hair was starting to curl as it dried, with little wisps falling in her face even though she kept shoving them back.

"Usually men quake in their boots when I walk by," she noted casually. "I have quite the reputation for being terrifying at work."

"Ah, but we're not talking about work, remember? And not your real name, or life, or politics, or headlines."

At her own words repeated back, her lips curved. "You're not a local. You don't have the slow Southern ways. And you don't have the accent, either, that lazy, drawn-out way of speaking that makes so many women want to swoon."

He sent her a lazy, drawn-out smile and drawled in a perfect imitation of an Alabama local, "I can make up the accent, if it'd make you swoon."

"Is it real?"

"The smile? Or the accent?"

"Either."

"Are you trying to charm me out of my panties?"

"You have quite a memory," she said, but smiled at her own expense. "I'll have to quit giving you things to make fun of me with."

"I wasn't making fun," Mike assured her. "Much."

"Hmm." She studied him with a sidelong glance. "You've very neatly avoided telling me if you're a local or not."

"Maybe your need for anonymity tonight goes both ways." Without thinking, he lifted a hand and stroked her cheek.

At the contact, she went utterly still, as if his touch had stunned her every bit as much as it had stunned him. And it *had* stunned him. He'd touched plenty of women in his life, some he'd known no longer than he'd known her, but never had his entire body quivered at that touch as it did now.

She searched his gaze long and hard, as if assessing him for something very important. Maybe…honesty?

He *was* being honest. Here, amid the crowd, sitting with the most arresting woman in the place, he didn't want to think about work, either. He didn't want to think about anything other than what he was doing, which was enjoying the company of a beautiful stranger.

She seemed to come to a conclusion about him. She nodded thoughtfully, then uncrossed her legs. Her stockings made the most arresting silk-on-silk sound, and for the longest moment he couldn't get his mind wrapped around anything but the thought of what her legs would feel like without the stockings. "Another drink?" he asked.

"That's how a good number of the people in here are going to get in trouble tonight." She glanced around. "Look at those women. Lonely. Drinking. Easy prey for all those men watching them."

"Maybe they want to be prey."

A sigh escaped her, a sound of…longing? "Yes," she said, so softly he had to lean closer. "Maybe so. Maybe they don't know how to just go after what they need, even if it's not practical."

"Are we talking about sex?" He grinned as she raised an eyebrow. "Because really, sex can be quite practical. It's a great stress reliever, for one.

And spectacular exercise. Not to mention it's just a feel-good sort of thing."

Her lips quirked. "You're speaking from experience, of course."

"Oh, no. A man should never kiss and tell."

That made her laugh, and she looked surprised at the rusty sound, as if she didn't do it often. "I need to get a room," she decided, slapping her palm on the bar as she reached for the bag she'd dropped at her feet. "There was a crowd at the front desk before."

He glanced at the very large—and getting larger by the moment—throng of people. "You don't have a room yet?"

"No, I wanted to get warm before standing in line."

Which was the last thing she said before the lights went out.

"DON'T PANIC," came the low, unbearably sexy voice of her perfect stranger. "I've got you."

And he did. He'd slid off his bar stool to stand right beside her, his hand reaching for hers. Corrine could feel the heat of him, the strength in the tall, leanly muscled body that she'd been trying not to notice since he'd first spoken to her.

He wasn't her type.

Which was damn laughable, because it had been so long, she didn't actually remember what her type was. At work, a man with a cocky, knowing smile and such a laid-back manner would drive her crazy.

But here it was the opposite.

At work she was serious, intense, and...okay, a perfectionist. She freely admitted that. She wasn't a sexual creature, not at all. In fact, working as a woman in a man's world, she tended to ignore her sexuality and the needs that went along with it, for long periods of time.

Hell of a time for her libido to lift its head.

"The power will come back on in a moment," he reassured her as everyone around them seemed to panic. "Nothing to be worried about."

Corrine wasn't worried, and it wasn't just his bone-melting voice making it so, but the fact that she didn't worry about things out of her control. It was a supreme waste of time, and she hated wasting anything, especially time.

Someone trying to get out of the bar jostled her. She wouldn't even be in this madhouse if she hadn't had to fly here from Houston for an emergency meeting of the utmost importance—meeting the new pilot. After this she could only hope there weren't any delays in her next project—commanding upcoming space shuttle mission STS-124. As it was her team would have to work hard to bring the replacement pilot on board.

Given the angry, disturbed, upset voices around her, general panic seemed imminent, so Corrine both forgave and ignored the person who'd pushed her. But she didn't intend to be pushed again.

"I'm going to make my way to the front desk," she said, turning her head toward where she imagined her stranger's ear would be. Making herself heard in the uproar was difficult. "I'm going to get a room and just sleep the power outage away—" *Oh God.* Her mouth brushed skin. *His ear*, she thought, but it was hard to think at all because her body tingled with the most mind-numbing awareness.

Lust.

She recognized it, cataloguing the fact in her technical mind. But it didn't stop the phenomenon.

"I'll come with you." That was all he said, but in the dark, his voice seemed even lower, even more husky and sexy, if possible. Before she could figure out how to lose him, he'd taken her bag and was tugging her toward the door.

There wasn't much light. None from the windows, which looked out into the pitch-black, stormy night. But since the generator hadn't kicked on, the bartender had lit candles along the length of the bar, and was doing her best to calm people down.

With her hand in the stranger's large, warm one, Corrine followed. An odd thing, following, something she as a leader didn't often do. But this man seemed to be a leader, as well, and she let him muscle his way through the mass of people. She had to admit, in a very sexist sort of way, that walking behind had its advantages. First of all, he smelled delicious, all woodsy and male. And second, even in the dark she could make out his broad shoulders and strong back. If only the light was slightly better, she could check out his—

"Uh-oh," he said, turning around so abruptly she plowed into him. He slipped one of his hands to her waist, holding her upright with ease as she caught her balance. "Looks like quite a few people beat us to the punch."

He was right.

Here in the lobby of the hotel, candles and battery lanterns cast an almost surreal light. The receptionist had a long line of people in front of her, and she looked harried, harassed and near hysteria.

In less than three minutes, the line started to dissipate. Far too quickly. Around them the grumbling increased, mimicking the force of the storm outside, as the wind and rain slashed against the walls, making it nearly impossible to hear.

Nearly.

"They're out of rooms," groaned the woman in front of them. "Now what?"

Corrine listened to the storm ravaging the hotel, and shivered. The thought of going back out there and finding another place to stay really irritated her, because damn it, she'd just started to dry off. That she'd told her assistant not to bother with reservations for the one night until her barracks room was ready was coming back to haunt her now. She marched up to the desk. "I want a room," she said coolly to the now teary receptionist.

The woman merely hiccuped.

Corrine briefly entertained the idea of ordering the woman to get a grip, that she should be helping people find other rooms in other hotels, or at the very least, looking sure and confident so people would stop yelling at her, but there was no point. "Check one more time," she said instead, in that voice of authority that always had people cracking. "I'll take anything."

Next to her, her stranger stirred, setting a hand very lightly on the base of her spine. At the touch, Corrine's every nerve leaped to attention and turned her knees wobbly.

"I don't think she has anything," he said quietly in her ear, causing all sorts of tremors inside her belly and other, far more erogenous, zones. "Or if she does, she's too worked up to find it."

Corrine sighed and nearly melted into the hand that was lightly, so lightly, rubbing the aching spot at the base of her spine. She caught herself just short of purring, and straightened, locking her traitorous knees while she was at it. "I know." She looked toward the double doors that led out into the night.

They opened and more people pushed their way in, seeking shelter. Rain and wind pelted everyone within ten feet of the doors. "It's back out there, then," she said with a shiver. "To find another place." She'd have to get a cab first, which wouldn't be easy in this weather. She'd be wet to the bone within two seconds. The thought wasn't appealing, but she had no choice and wasn't one to cry over spilled milk.

Intending to bid her stranger goodbye, she turned to him, but he spoke first.

"I have a room," he said very softly. "And I'm happy to share it with you."

2

CORRINE STARED at her perfect stranger, shocked. Although it was dark all around them, she could feel his searching gaze on her, like a caress. In the depths of his warm, blessedly dry jacket, she shivered.

Not from the cold now, but from something far more complicated.

Another woman joined the nervous young receptionist behind the desk. "I'm the manager," she said to Corrine. "We're terribly sorry for the inconvenience, but as you can see, with no power and the generator not operating properly, we're in no position to get you a room or help you find another place. You can wait the storm out here in the lobby or make your own arrangements."

Wait the storm out? In this cold, dark, noisy room with all these other unhappy people?

Or she could hike back out there and try to catch a cab.

Some choice.

The man behind her stirred, just enough to have his thigh brush the back of hers, and everything inside her went still, then hot.

He'd offered his room.

And his bed.

Probably his body, too.

Please, her own body begged her brain. *Oh, pretty, pretty please.*

"Ma'am?" The manager looked at Corrine, impatience shimmering. She had other people to cater to at the moment, to smile at and try to appease.

What to do?

Corrine had been born to rule. Just ask her parents, who'd called her Queen Bee since day one. Her mom, a biochemist, and her father, a cardiologist, joked that it was in her genetic makeup to be the boss.

Corrine had to admit she'd lived up to their predictions.

Maybe if she'd been raised by people who hadn't understood her, who hadn't encouraged her to do whatever she wanted to do, be whatever she wanted to be, she might have turned out to be a holy terror, but truthfully, she wasn't spoiled at all. Shortly after her family had moved to Houston when she was a child, she'd dreamed of becoming an astronaut. She worked damn hard for what she wanted, and never gave up until she got it. No matter if it was being high school valedictorian, or graduating from college a year early, or entering the Manned Space Flight Program at NASA because she was determined to fly space shuttles. She'd not only entered, but had succeeded beyond everyone's expectations.

Except her own, that is.

Thanks to unwavering tenacity, sheer stubbornness and damned hard work, she'd risen through the ranks, flown on a record four missions to date as pilot, and was now going to be only the third woman in history to command a mission.

So maybe she was confident. And okay, a little tough. But to make it in space and aeronautics, traditionally run by men, she had to be. Corrine knew she used that toughness to purposely scare and intimidate the people around her, but she'd never have made it so far if she hadn't.

In that spirit, she considered demanding a staff room, but something happened. The man's fingers, still on her waist, spread wide now, his thumb skimming over her side, then her belly, making the muscles there quiver like crazy.

"I have a room," he said again quietly, her perfect stranger. Her perfect, mouthwateringly gorgeous stranger, who had an unbelievably sexy voice, with sexy eyes, sexy hands and an even sexier body to go with it.

What his fingers were doing to her system should have been illegal. She could no longer even see straight, she was so consumed with lust for this man, who was more handsome than the devil, thrillingly rough around the edges and full of promised sin. He had a slow, sensual smile that lit up the night. He was intelligent, humorous, and he wanted to share his room with her.

"What do you think?" he asked.

That she was crazy. That she had an intensely structured, controlled schedule for the next months. She was too mature for this.

Too…busy.

Oh damn, but that sounded pretentious. Why couldn't it be simple? Why couldn't she be as entitled to one night of frivolity as anyone else? She'd been too long without this sort of connection, and she deserved it, deserved one night of pure selfishness and pleasure, where no one would bow to her, kowtow to her commands or try to brownnose. She was entitled to be a woman once in a while.

Wasn't she?

As calmly as possible, she turned back to the manager, on the off chance this had all been some mistake.

But the woman was shaking her head. "I'm sorry."

The relief Corrine felt surprised her, but she was always honest, maybe to a fault. In light of that, she had to admit, at least to herself, that she didn't really want a way out of this. She'd flown into Huntsville to deal with an emergency. Whatever it was, it was big, and it would affect both her and the space-shuttle mission she'd lived and breathed for a year and a half now.

For these remaining months she wouldn't have any time to herself. None. This was it. This one last night.

It scared her how much she wanted it.

Turning in the dark, she bumped into his chest, and could tell by his quick, indrawn breath that she affected him every bit as much as he affected her. *Silly*, she wanted to tell him. *Juvenile. We're acting like hormonal teenagers.*

His fingers played again at the base of her spine. And all those hormones unleashed by her own hunger leaped and jerked within her. Breathing became optional. She wanted to melt to the floor in a boneless heap of jelly.

It should have been embarrassing. Awkward, at the very least. There should have been fear and doubt, for a million different reasons; that she didn't even know his name should have led the pack.

Instead, the strangest feeling of...*rightness* flooded her.

In the dark she craned her neck, trying to see his face clearly. She couldn't, and she felt more than actually saw his slow, easy smile.

Everything inside her reacted, helplessly.

Oh yeah. She was absolutely in the right place with the right man. "Yes," she said.

"Yes?"

She inhaled deeply. "Yes, I'd like to share your room."

The receptionist and manager had both leaned close to hear her answer, and then looked like maybe they wanted to cry in relief. "His key will work," the manager said. "The electronic keying system is on emergency power and is one of the few things actually operating right now. You'll have no problem getting into the room."

Behind them, the crowd was growing impatient.

Her perfect stranger, who smelled like heaven and had a touch nearly as divine, didn't say a word, just took her hand, lifted it to his lips and then, still holding on to her, took the lead.

And for the second time that night, and for only the second time in her entire life, she followed.

MORE THAN ONCE in his life Mike had been accused of being cocky and confident, yet laid-back and easygoing. Sometimes downright lazy.

But as anyone who'd ever worked with him could attest, he was actually a very controlled man. It wasn't often he lost that control, but he nearly did now. He had an incredibly beautiful woman by the hand and was taking her to his room, and he had no idea what she expected.

The guys would laugh hysterically at that, he knew, for Mike had quite the reputation, especially when it came to women.

But the truth was, much of that bad-boy rep

was hype, at least in the past few years, when he'd been far too busy to live up to it.

Through the dark, he glanced at her over his shoulder and found her watching him. He squeezed her hand and smiled.

She returned both the squeeze and the smile, and his body actually twitched with excitement. With any luck at all, his fantasy and reality were going to commingle tonight.

They crossed the large, noisy lobby carefully, winding their way through the unsettled crowd.

"Are *all* these people stranded?" she wondered aloud.

Mike didn't stop, but squeezed her hand again. "Looks like it."

"This is terrible."

It was, and he felt badly, too, but not enough to invite more up to share his room. In the midst of work, work, work, he'd somehow found a little something for himself. Frivolous. Dangerous even, considering the day and age and all the problems associated with recreational sex, but there was something about this woman that told him she was different.

A soft glow from various lanterns and candles lit the way to the elevators, which of course weren't working. There were people there, too, staring with dismay at the closed doors.

Mike's room was on the sixth floor.

It could have been worse, far worse. "We have to take the stairs," he said regretfully, pulling her up beside him. He felt bad, though not for himself. Given the physical demands of his job, not to mention the rigorous training he was constantly put through, he could take the stairs in two minutes without breaking a sweat.

But she wouldn't find it so easy. Her wet skirt, while not skimpy by any means, had to be confining, and those heels…well, they showed off her mouthwatering legs, but they couldn't be comfortable. In the dim light, her damp hair shone. Her skin did, too, along with her eyes, which were filled with deep, dark mysteries. "Six flights of stairs," he added apologetically.

She murmured noncommittally.

"We'll take it slow," he assured her, and could have sworn she laughed. But when he peered through the dark at her face, she was smiling slightly.

"Ready when you are," she said.

When he opened the door to the stairwell, an inky blackness greeted them. To reassure the woman next to him, he once again took her hand. "Don't worry," he said, pulling from his pocket a pen that was also a flashlight. When he flicked it on, she looked at him in surprise.

"You actually carry a flashlight? In your pocket?"

Yes, he carried a flashlight. And a hand-held electronic organizer. And a state-of-the-art cell phone that could download from the net and retrieve his e-mail. He was a techno-geek and couldn't help himself, but in his defense, he'd spent years and years in Russia, far from his home country. His toys somehow made him feel closer.

"You must be an engineer," she decided.

"I am not."

Her lips were curved, her eyes lit with humor, and she was so beautiful she took his breath away.

"Are you sure?" She was still teasing. "Now that I think about it, you look like one."

"Do you really want to know?" he asked softly, suddenly wanting to tell her about himself, wanting to hear all about her in return. It was silly, dangerous even, because with that additional emotional connection, he knew whatever they shared this night was bound to be the most powerful affair he'd ever had.

She stared at him, searched deep in his eyes for God knew what. And then, finally, she shook her head. "It's tempting," she whispered regretfully, lifting her hand to gently touch his mouth. "But no. I don't want to know."

For a long moment he didn't move, hoping, wishing she'd change her mind, but then the moment passed and he forced a smile. "I like to be prepared," he said, directing the flashlight ahead of them. *And please, God, let me be "prepared" with a condom in my shaving kit.*

"Prepared." She let out a little laugh, again a slightly rusty sound, as if she didn't do it often, and he smiled back.

Make that a box of condoms, he thought.

They started up the stairs. At the top of the first flight, Mike paused. "Need a rest?"

"After one flight of stairs?" She shook her head. "Tell me I don't look that fragile to you."

She was petite but not frail, not with all those wonderful curves and a face so full of life. "You don't look fragile to me," he said after a good long look that stirred his body.

"Smart answer."

They climbed another flight, and when Mike again paused at the top, she lifted a brow. "Do *you* need to rest?"

He smiled and they started on the next flight, but at a burst of wild laughter ahead of them, he once again slowed to a stop. Sprawled across the stairs, two men were sharing a flask of what had to be pretty potent stuff, given their wide, slack, idiotic grins.

"Looksy there," one said, slurring his words as he nudged the man next to him. "Now that's the way to pass the time, matey." The drunk leered at Mike and gave an exaggerated wink. "Don't need to tell you to keep warm, huh? You've got your heating blankie right there with you."

Both men laughed uproariously, and as they did, slipped down a few stairs, to fall together in a heap. It made them laugh even harder.

"Feeling no pain, I see." Mike stepped over them and helped her do the same.

The next flight of stairs began the same way, but then they heard a strange, heated moaning, then rapid panting. Mike didn't know what he expected to find. A fight, maybe. Someone stabbed or shot, someone in labor...he couldn't tell from the frightening sounds. He was prepared for anything, though, and tried to keep the woman behind him to protect her.

But she refused to be kept there, even for her own good. She evaded his hands and stayed stubbornly by his side.

The sounds came from a couple, and it wasn't a fight or severe wounds, as he'd feared, but a wild mating. Clothes were half torn off both of them. They were writhing together against the wall, and given the scream of pleasure that tore from the woman's lips, they were also deep in the throes of orgasm.

Mike looked at "Lola," but she didn't close her eyes or seem embarrassed. She just stared at the couple in front of them, as if mesmerized.

They had a perfect view. The woman was wedged up against the wall; the man could touch and grab at will, which he was doing. Her breasts were bare, and bouncing wildly in the man's face, which elicited plenty of encouraging groans from both of them. His hands snaked up her skirt, where he held her hips so that he could thrust into her, time and time again.

"Now! Now!" she shrieked. "Oh, Billy, *now!*"

"Yeah," said Billy as he pounded into her. "Yeah, baby."

"Ohh." Breasts jiggled. Her bottom bounced. Skin slapped against skin. "Oh, Billy, I'm going to come again!"

"Yeah, baby. Me, too."

Together they let out more shrieks and cries, and then moaning gutturally, they slumped together.

The woman standing next to Mike let out a strangled sound of her own. "Can we get past them, do you think?"

She sounded…breathless, and her palm in his had gotten warm. Almost sweaty.

Mike knew the feeling. He had never considered himself voyeuristic, but witnessing this couple, with Lola beside him, his desire kicked up a degree. He was so hot, so hard and so unbelievably ready he could hardly nod. "Come on," he muttered, and together the two of them started running.

Up the fifth flight, then the sixth.

At the top, Mike stopped, certain he'd gone too fast this time.

"If you ask me if I need to rest," she said seriously, "I will smack you."

She wasn't even winded. Neither was he, but hell, they'd come a long way up.

"And if you marvel about what good shape I'm in," she continued, "when you're obviously in just as good a shape, I'll—"

"I know," he said. "Smack me. Don't worry, I'll restrain myself and admire your strength later. Come on."

They made it to his door. No one was around, and the hallway was pitch-black except for the light from his trusty flashlight.

Taking out his key card, he looked down into her face. She was watching him with an unreadable expression. Slowly he reached out and stroked a finger over her cheek, her jaw. "Are you sure?"

"Already sorry you asked me?"

"Are you kidding?"

"Well then, I'm not sorry I'm here." She lifted a hand, too, and touched his face, ran her finger over his lower lip, over his jaw so that his day-old growth of beard rasped loudly in the silent hall. When she rimmed his ear, he sucked in a harsh breath, every muscle tight and tense.

"Are we going to stand out here all night?" she asked. "Or go in and…"

"And?" he pressed, stepping closer and running his fingers down her neck now, delighting in the shiver that wracked her. He stroked his thumb over the pulse dancing wildly at the base of her throat.

"And finish this," she whispered, her eyes closing, her head falling back slightly to give him more room. "Let's finish what we started the moment we looked into each other's eyes. Okay?"

"Oh yeah. It's more than okay." And with his body—and heart—buzzing, he put his key card in the slot.

3

THE ROOM SEEMED DARKER than the hallway. Dark but warm, and somehow inviting.

Definitely their safe haven from the storm.

Corrine stepped into the room and moved silently to the window. Pulling back the shades didn't let more light into the room. The blurry window was streaming with rain and sleet, but this high up, with the windows sealed, the night and the storm were eerily silent. She could barely make out the city below, and it was easy to believe they were anywhere, anywhere in the world, all alone.

He came up behind her, not touching, just…there. "I'm not married," he said. "Or attached." When she craned her neck and looked at him, he gave a little smile. "I know, you don't want to talk about yourself, and you don't want to talk about me, either, but I just wanted you to know that."

She had a hard time imagining this man without companionship. "You're unattached?"

He shrugged. "I see women. Nothing serious has come my way. Not yet, anyway."

She was selfishly relieved. She'd never been married, and hadn't been attached in so long she'd almost forgotten what it was like. Oddly enough, given such a lack of romance, Corrine's life was made up of men. But even being with men on a daily basis, she'd never been more aware of one in her life than she was right now. She felt surrounded by him, her perfect stranger, and she shivered again, though it had nothing to do with fear or intimidation or cold, everything to do with stark, demanding need.

If that need hadn't been so strong, so undeniable, so utterly reciprocated, she would have died of embarrassment, because Corrine Atkinson didn't need anyone, never had. But it *was* strong, it *was* undeniable and it was most definitely reciprocated. "I'm not married or attached, either," she said, turning toward him. "If nothing else, you deserve to know that."

His smile was slow and nearly stopped her heart. "Good," he said.

More lightning flashed, but the thunder was

muted, almost as if it was happening in another time and place.

"I love to watch a storm," she said, suddenly nervous enough to let him in, just a little. "Especially at night."

"It's different at night," he agreed. "More intense. When you can't see, the other senses kick in, so you feel it more."

Exactly. He understood.

Which caused even more nervousness. "My mother hates this weather. It messes with her hair." *Where had that come from?* Corrine never shared herself, any part, including her family. To share meant opening up, and that wasn't her way.

Before she could cover up that slip with a light joke, he stroked her hair. "It only makes yours all the more beautiful."

Uncomfortable with compliments, she lifted a hand to the long, tangled mess, which had gone wild the moment she'd stepped out of the cab.

"I love the curls," he said, and stroked it again.

She felt the touch to the tips of her toes. "I usually keep it confined." Another personal fact, damn it. Her hair was one of those things about herself that she'd change if she could, like webbed feet or short, fat fingers. "I leave it long because I can pin it back. If I cut it short I look like a mop."

He laughed.

Good Lord, who'd given her tongue permission to run off with her mouth?

"It's so soft." He tucked a particularly wayward curl behind her ear, his fingers tracing down along her jaw.

She could no longer breathe.

His hand danced down her throat to the lapels of his jacket, which he drew more tightly together.

He thought she was cold.

The gentleness of this man floored her, along with his size and shape and his utterly confident masculine air.

"I can sleep on the floor," he said quietly, and the tenderness in his voice, combined with the careful way he was touching her, nearly did her in.

"No, I—"

He put a hand to his chest. "I wanted you here more than I wanted my next breath, but now that you are here, I don't want to rush you."

She stared at his hand, but that wasn't what

drew her eyes, not really. It was his chest, which was broad, muscled and calling for her hands.

She tried to remember the last time she'd been drawn to a man, but couldn't. She saw attractive men all the time, and not one of them had ever sparked an interest in her.

This man wasn't causing just a spark, he'd started a full-blown wildfire, and it wasn't simply his physical beauty, though that was nothing to sneeze at. It wasn't his smile, though that alone had been enough to set her hormones raging.

There was just something about him, so big and tough, yet so…gentle.

He'd probably laugh at that, or maybe get embarrassed. And yet again, maybe not; he seemed to be a man embarrassed by very little.

"You're not rushing me," she finally said.

He flashed his smile, then set his hands on her shoulders and turned her away from him again. In what started out as a light, sexy touch, he kneaded, then found the knot of tension at the base of her neck that she was rarely without these days. With a rough sound of empathy, he dug in.

She nearly melted to the floor, unable to contain her soft moan of pleasure as his fingers unerringly zeroed in on the place she needed them most.

"Mmm, you're so tight. Try to relax a bit." He smoothed the muscles all the way down her arms and out toward her fingertips, then started again at her neck. He did that, over and over, with infinite patience, until she had to grip the windowsill to keep from sliding to the floor in a boneless heap of massive gratification.

"Better?"

"If it gets any better," she said, "I just might explode."

"Promise?" As if rendering a woman completely out of control was an everyday occurrence for him, he laughed huskily when she let out another helpless little moan.

And it well might be for him, but not for her. Certainly not for her. When was the last time she'd had sex? She tried to remember, but his fingers were working their magic and now she could feel his chest, his thighs, brushing her back and legs, making her even weaker.

"It's very late," she said.

His fingers stilled, then he carefully stepped back. "Yes, it is. You'll want to go to sleep."

She turned to him, her heart in her throat. "I think maybe this is worth being tired for."

He'd been wearing a solemn expression, but now she saw what he'd been hiding behind that in case she turned him down. Stark desire and need, even fear—everything she was feeling was in his gaze, and there was no way she could resist it, no way she wanted to.

She'd given herself this night, and she wasn't going to take it back now. But even in their anonymity, there was something they had to discuss. "I don't have any protection." She actually blushed; she hadn't done that since grade school. "I wasn't...expecting this."

His smile was sweet and self-deprecatory. "Neither was I. I'm just hoping that in my shaving kit I still have... Hold on." He vanished into the bathroom, and she saw the quick small flash of his penlight. Then he was back, relief shining in his strong features as he held up two condoms.

"Two." She went a little weak in the knees. "Well..." She was actually breathless. "It's rumored two of anything is better than one, right?"

He let out a low laugh, then his mouth brushed her cheek. She turned toward him. Their lips connected once, then again, making her sigh. "You taste just the way you smell," she murmured, not really meaning to say it out loud. "Like heaven."

A sound escaped him, one that might have been humor mixed in with hunger, and slowly, slowly, he eased his jacket off her shoulders before drawing her close and moving her against him.

She nearly died of delight right then and there, because his body was large and hard and so thrilling she tipped her head back and wordlessly asked him to kiss her again.

He did, but she needed more. She had since she'd first set eyes on him, and it wasn't entirely loneliness now, but a hunger she'd never experienced before.

Cupping her face, he continued to kiss her, more deeply now, touching her as if she were special, precious. Feminine.

She wanted to be all those things to a man, *this* man, if only for a night. He fascinated her. He was beautiful and physical. He was dangerous, if only to her mental health. And he was hard and aroused, for her.

Perfect.

She wrapped her arms around his neck at the same time he caught her up against him. His mouth was firm, demanding in a quiet way that reminded her of his voice. But he didn't press her for more than that simple connection of their mouths, and she realized that he wouldn't.

If she wanted more, which she most definitely did, she would have to take it. It wasn't that he didn't want her in turn; she could feel that he did, could feel the satisfying bulge between his powerful thighs. And his restraint made her want him all the more.

Later she would wonder what had come over her during that dark, stormy night, but for now, safe in his warm, strong, giving arms, there seemed no better way to satisfy the emptiness deep inside her. "More," she said, sinking her fingers into his hair, lifting his head to look deeply into his melting brown eyes.

"More," he promised. Still holding her, he turned toward the bed.

She felt a moment's hesitation when he laid her on the sheets, but then he pulled off his clothes. Oh, how she wished there was light. But when he set a knee on the bed, then crawled toward her, she was able to catch sight of his incredible body and forgot everything else. His chest was broad, tapered down to a flat belly that she itched to touch. His thighs were long, taut with strength, and between them, he was hard and heavy.

Fully aroused.

He was a stranger, so that nothing about any part of him was familiar, yet she lifted her arms and welcomed him closer as if they'd known each other forever. His mouth took hers, more hungrily this time, and his hunger fueled hers. As if it needed fueling!

The heat spread, and when he undid her blouse, and then her bra, gliding both off her shoulders, she found herself panting, her hips already pressing insistently toward his. He excited her beyond belief, and if she could think, which she definitely couldn't, she might have been horrified at her lack of control.

And yet it never occurred to her to stop him, not then, and not when he slid the rest of her clothes off and his condom on. Not when he cupped her face in his big hands and kissed her, deep and wet and long. And certainly not when he touched her first with his eyes, then his fingers, then his mouth, and then finally, oh finally, sank into her.

Outside, the storm continued to rage, while inside one of not such a different nature took its course, as well. Reality had little chance, between the flashes of lightning and the flashes of bare, naked hunger. The friction of his thrusts and the greed of her own body shattered her. It might have been terrifying, how far he lifted her out of herself, if he hadn't been right there with her. She was still in the throes of a shockingly powerful orgasm—her third!—when he buried his face in her hair and found his own release.

MORNING WAS BOUND TO COME, Corrine knew, but damn it, did it have to arrive so soon?

Bright orange-and-yellow rays of sunlight filtered through the crack in the curtains, casting an almost surreal light in the room, assuring her that the storm had passed.

Definitely, morning. And with it, responsibilities.

Damn.

She lay in the embrace of her perfect stranger. They were both deliciously, gloriously naked, pressed skin to skin, heat to heat. For an indulgent moment she just looked at him as he slept on, at all his masculine beauty, wondering at the hard, leanly muscled body that had brought her to paradise and back so many times in the night.

His eyes were closed, his face relaxed, his chest rising and falling evenly. His firm mouth brought back memories of what he could do with it, and made her body tingle all over. His lashes were dark, long and thick, resting against his strong cheekbone. His jaw had darkened with stubble, the same stubble that had rasped so satisfyingly over her skin all night long.

He was curled around her, one arm gallantly being used as her pillow, the other tightly anchoring her to him. His fingers cradled her breast possessively. From this angle, she couldn't see much below his waist, but she could feel him pressed to her, every delicious, rock-hard inch of him. She sighed with pleasure. He was amazingly tough, strong, hard in all the right places, and so beautiful it almost hurt.

Just looking at him made her heart contract. He was someone she could have allowed herself to care for, if she ever allowed such things. But she couldn't, at least not now, not with her all-consuming mission coming up. Some other time, perhaps…

Though she knew that was a lie. She'd always told herself that someday she'd allow Prince

Charming into her life, but the timing was never right.

But damn it, when? *When* would it be right?

Her heart constricted again, but she ignored it. In her not-so-humble opinion, she had it all, the way her life was right at this moment. She had great parents who supported her incredibly busy lifestyle, and she had the best job in the world.

True, she didn't have her *own* family, not a husband or children, but she didn't have time for that. She did have needs, like any other normal, red-blooded woman, but those needs were easily met. When she felt the occasional itch, she went out and got it scratched. Carefully, of course, but she wasn't shy.

Just like last night.

And now she would go on with her life. Content. Happy. Fulfilled.

Just as she wanted to.

So why, then, didn't she extract herself? Why did she lie there panting after a man who should have been out of her system by dawn's first light? She couldn't say for certain, but reflecting on the matter would have to come another time.

She had to go.

Slipping out from beneath his arm wasn't easy,

but she was a master at stealth. Still, she couldn't help thinking *If he wakes up now, it's fate.* No way could she look into those warm, inviting eyes and walk away. Especially if he flashed that equally warm, inviting smile and reached for her, which she imagined him doing, then imagined her own open-armed response…

He didn't budge.

Tempting fate, she leaned in close, softly kissed his cheek.

I'll never forget you.

For a moment she stood by the bed, yearning and longing for something she couldn't put a name to. But even if she could, it was no use.

She was simply no good at matters of the heart. Dressing quickly and quietly, she hesitated one last time at the door.

Then, picking up her bag, she finally left, knowing she had no choice. No choice at all.

4

AS ALWAYS, Mike slept like the dead and awoke by degrees. It was a great fault of his, being so slow to shake sleep. Over the years he'd gotten both ribbed about it and in real trouble, not the least of which was the time he'd slept through his first "SIM"—space shuttle simulation pilot test. He'd been in Russia, and had just battled a week-long flu, which he'd kept silent about so as not to have to give up the chance. The test had been agonizingly long, and his "landing" required a pre-dawn wakeup. Thanks to his cold medications, he hadn't made it, and as a result, the autopilot had kicked in for the simulated event, "demolishing" the entire landing strip and center, "killing" over one hundred people.

That particular mishap had caused him years of jokes at his expense, not to mention requiring some serious kissing up. He'd practically had to beg to be kept in the program.

And now, when he finally managed to crack his eyes open, and saw the bright sunlight pouring in through the hotel window, he knew before reaching out that he was alone.

Still he stretched, touching her side of the pillow they'd shared when they hadn't been rolling, tangled and heated and breathless, across the sheets.

It was cold.

She'd been gone for a while then, and he had no one to blame but himself for the odd mixture of real regret and not so real relief.

As he rose and showered, Mike reminded himself that he had no time in his life for any serious entanglements. Having to fill in for this mission as pilot, when the mission had been in the planning stages for so long, meant he had months of catching up to do. He knew better than to think it would be a piece of cake. It was going to take every single second of every single day until launch to pull this off.

First, he had to get through the initial process of inserting himself into an already established team. They were in Huntsville to immerse themselves in this critical project. In a week, they'd move on to Houston, where they would stay until launch time, with occasional trips back and forth to Kennedy Space Center in Florida.

He was looking at a whirlwind of activity.

Which meant this was not the time to be considering a personal attachment. That was actually a good thing, as he'd never wanted a personal attachment.

But last night, what he'd shared with that woman…now *that* could have been the first time he might have actually paused and considered anything close to a relationship.

But she was gone, and he had to work, so it was over.

Which didn't explain why after his shower he stood staring down at the rumpled bed, yearning and burning for something just out of his reach.

He dressed and ate as if it was just any other morning, and everything was normal. Same old, same old.

But it wasn't. He wasn't.

He knew he had last night to thank for that. He'd known from the moment she'd set foot in that bar, soaking wet, head high and eyes bright, that she was going to shake things up.

She'd done that and more; she'd shaken him to the core. He tried not to think about that, and also about what he could have felt for her, under different circumstances.

How could that happen, he wondered, after only a little conversation and some good sex?

Okay, *great* sex.

Regardless, it wasn't like him to be mooning on the morning after. He'd always been the one running. But *she'd* left *him*, without a word or note, and he would have sworn that's exactly what he wanted.

So why was he entertaining other thoughts, about things like relationships and family and white picket fences? He had missions to fly and hopefully someday command. A wife and kids sounded nice, but for far, far, *far* down the road. Not now.

At 0900 hours on the dot, he entered the Marshall Flight Center. He expected to leap right into work, expected to be whisked into the whole rush of it immediately.

He didn't expect a conference room filled with smiling people and good food—usually an oxymoron when it came to government-provided meals.

Though he'd spent very little time in the United States since his Air Force days, many of

the people milling around were familiar to him.
The space industry was like that—very incestu-
ous. Even during the Cold War, when politicians
from one country wouldn't speak to, or even recognize, politicians from another, science had
managed to remain universal. As countries, Russia and the United States might have ignored
each other for years, but their scientists hadn't.
They'd been sharing the designing and planning
of expeditions and experiments since the very beginning, and nothing had changed since.

Few people on the outside realized how closely
Russia, Japan, the United States and many other
countries were working together to build the International Space Station, and even now, just
thinking about it made Mike's chest swell with
pride at being a part of it.

"Welcome, Mike!"

He found his hand being energetically pumped
by Tom Banks, an old astronaut training buddy
who now worked in ground control. Mike was
surprised to see Tom had lost some hair and
gained some weight since those training days.

"I heard the good news!" Tom was grinning.
"You're back in the States, filling in for Patrick."
His smile faded. "Poor guy. Can't believe he

biffed it so badly parachuting. Sporting three pins in his leg, did you hear?"

"Ouch." Mike wondered exactly how selfish it was of him to be grateful for the miracle of that mishap, and also the fact that the backup pilot had contracted hepatitis.

Probably pretty damn selfish.

But he'd been training for exactly this opportunity for years. He'd been in space twice before and couldn't wait to get back up there. So far, all he knew was that the mission would carry and install the third of eight sets of solar arrays that, at the completion of construction in 2006, would comprise the space station's electrical power system, converting sunlight to usable energy. It was a project he was intimately familiar with, as he'd been working on it in Russia for years. "How is it all going?"

"It's going," Tom said, nodding. "They're thrilled to have you, as your reputation precedes you."

That, Mike knew, could be good or bad.

"Hey, heard about last year," Tom said. "How you limped back after the payload fire midflight."

Limped. Kind word for nearly losing it, as in

crashing back to earth, becoming fish food, biting the big one. Thanks to some quick thinking on Mike's part—and he was convinced anyone on that team could have done the same, he'd just gotten there first—he'd managed to contain the fire and put it out before it destroyed them beyond repair. "I don't care to repeat that experience," he said in grand understatement.

"You were a lucky bastard, that's for certain. All of you."

"Have you met your team?" Tom turned to the two men who'd just come up to them. "Mike Wright, meet Jimmy Westmoreland, Mission Specialist-One. And Frank Smothers, Mission Specialist-Two."

As it turned out, Mike had met both men before. They'd come to Russia several years back to study some of the communications equipment for the space station in its planning stages, so it was more of a reunion than anything else. A few moments later he was introduced to Stephen Philips, the fifth member of the team and their payload specialist.

"You've met everyone now," Tom said. "Not bad for your first ten minutes here."

"I haven't met the commander." Oddly

enough, Mike felt his first flash of...not apprehension; that was far too strong a word for a man who felt so utterly comfortable in his world. But just as the space industry was notorious for its small population of overeducated overachievers, it was also notorious for its big egos, and no one, absolutely no one, made it to commander status without a significant sense of self-importance.

Added to that was yet another problem.

This commander was a woman.

Everyone knew Mike loved women. He cherished them, dreamed about them, wanted them, enjoyed them.

Take last night, for example.

But working for a woman? As in, directly beneath one?

He didn't want to think of himself as biased or sexist, but honest to God, he couldn't imagine why a woman would want to be commander of the space shuttle, he just couldn't. It took strength, a tough-as-nails demeanor and, well, *balls.*

"Corrine Atkinson?" Stephen craned his neck, as did Tom and the others. Unlike Tom, Frank, Jimmy and Stephen were of average height or taller, and leanly muscular. They wore the short,

short buzz cut that screamed military, and all of them had the look of tough, rigidly controlled, well-trained athletes.

Unfortunately, astronauts on the whole were not nearly as serious-minded as their reputation might lead the general public to believe. In fact, for the most part they were great pranksters and troublemakers, not one of these guys being an exception.

"The commander is here somewhere," Stephen assured Mike. "She just came in from Houston."

"She flew in to meet you, in fact," Frank said, far too innocently. He ruined it by grinning. "Don't worry. We told her all about you."

Jimmy joined in with his own evil grin. "Yeah. We started with that time we came to Russia and you brought us to that party, remember?"

God help him, he did.

"And those women jumped out of a cake," Jimmy added, though Mike already knew the rest.

"They were some great lookers," Frank said. "But then we found out they were prostitutes. You tried to send them home, Mike, remember? They didn't have a ride, so we offered to give them one—"

Mike groaned at the recounting of the bachelor party for one of his comrades. "Tell me you didn't tell her this."

"Oh, yes. We did. She especially liked the next part." Frank grinned. "You remember...the naked part."

"Okay, that was *not* my fault." Mike rubbed his temples. "And when they pulled their guns to rob us, we didn't get hurt. Did you tell her that, I hope?"

"We were safe only because they had a crush on you," Jimmy pointed out. "They *still* took our wallets and cash."

"And our clothes," Frank added. "Don't forget they took our clothes and then our keys, and left us by the side of the road."

"It started to rain," Jimmy recalled with a shiver. "Hard."

"Yeah." Frank smiled in fond remembrance. "Good thing it wasn't winter."

"The commander," Mike said weakly. "She found that story particularly fascinating, I suppose."

"Oh, yeah."

Everyone but Mike doubled over with laughter.

Great. Just great. Mike hadn't even met the woman and he was probably on her shit list.

"There she is now," Stephen said, pointing across the room.

She had her back to them. All Mike could tell from the view was that she was rather petite. No other details, except she'd pulled her hair back in a severe bun that reminded him of Mrs. Stestlebaum, his strict, terrifying first-grade teacher.

Commander Corrine Atkinson appeared to favor boxy business suits that didn't show nearly enough of the female body to suit him, and hid any curves she might or might not have.

"Come on, I'll introduce you," Tom said.

Mike drew in a deep breath, feeling resigned, but not sure why. So she dressed a little stiffly. So she liked to torture her scalp with unforgiving hairdos. It didn't mean she would be difficult to work for.

He hoped.

"Mike?"

"Yeah," he said to Tom. "Coming." But he didn't move.

Frank laughed and slapped him on the back. "It's just the boss, big guy, not the guillotine."

But Mike knew that sometimes they could be

one and the same. Together, moving as a team already, they strode forward to introduce him, the other men smiling, relaxed in a way that suddenly Mike couldn't have imitated to save his life.

Strange, given how much he enjoyed smiling and being relaxed.

He didn't understand it, at least not until he got within two feet of her and she turned to face him.

CORRINE GOT THAT FUNNY tingle at the base of her skull, the one that warned her that something exciting—good or bad, she couldn't yet tell—was about to happen.

The inkling was right on, she discovered, as she slowly turned and faced the group of men standing there smiling, all of whom she knew, some better than others.

With the exception of the one in front.

Her perfect stranger.

The man with the wicked eyes and even more wicked hands, the one she imagined would headline her fantasies for years to come, was standing right there in front of her.

Only now he wasn't in worn jeans and a clean

T-shirt, sitting at the bar tapping his foot in tune with the music as a storm raged outside. Now he wasn't looking alone and sexy, and just a tad bit dangerous to her mental health.

Now he was…oh, definitely still sexy and just a tad bit dangerous to her mental health—but no longer alone late at night.

He was surrounded by her team, looking for all the world as if he belonged there, looking as if he'd been *born* there.

"Commander Atkinson? This is Mike Wright," Tom said proudly. "In the flesh."

Flesh. Oh, she knew his flesh. *Intimately.* And at just the thought, she blushed.

Blushed.

Unimaginable. She opened her mouth, maybe to deny this could really be happening, maybe just to let out an indignant squeak, but thankfully, he spoke first.

"*You're* the commander?" He looked as sick as she did. "Commander Atkinson?"

At least he was every bit as stunned as she. Which didn't help things, not one little bit, not when her perfect stranger was… Oh my God.

On her team.

He was a subordinate. He was going to have to

take direct orders from her, and as she knew damned well, he wouldn't like it. He was strong and tough and his own man…and this couldn't be happening, this couldn't really be happening.

She couldn't have accidentally slept with someone she was going to work closely with. God, *more* than closely, they were going to be practically glued at the hip for the next four months. This was some sort of cosmic joke. It had to be.

A nightmare.

For the first time in her life, she was truly speechless, with no idea of how to react.

But she could see he did. In fact, he was already reaching out his hand, not to shake hers as a stranger would, but to hold it and squeeze gently, in that very familiar way he had, a way that would scream to anyone watching what they'd been to each other, only hours before. "You're—"

"Mike. Mike Wright."

He had a name. Fancy that. She jerked her hand away and carefully schooled her features into a cool passivity. "Nice to meet you."

He wasn't only surprised at her civil tone and refusal to acknowledge that they knew each other, he looked shocked as well. But she couldn't register that at the moment; all she could think was...*he* was Mike Wright!

Not her first choice for pilot, or even her second, but those men had been taken from her by circumstance. When American-born and Russian-trained astronaut Mikhail Wright had been suggested for emergency secondary backup, she'd agreed, because his amazing talent and precise control were well known. Though she'd never met him, she'd thought he'd be perfect.

Perfect.

God, he was. He had been. And now she'd pay the price.

"It was very good of you to leave Russia and your projects there to come join our team," she said evenly. "Thank you."

He just stared at her.

"Well..." Her voice trailed off, because for just a moment she wasn't the commander, but Corrine the woman, the one who'd let a man in, and because of that had seen possibilities she couldn't imagine.

The situation couldn't be worse. Well, okay, actually it could; everyone in the room could know she'd slept with him.

That would be worse.

If her team found out, she'd lose her tough, intense edge, at least in their eyes. All her control would be taken away, and much of their respect, and that would be a fate worse than death because of how hard she'd worked to get where she was.

Straightening both her spine and her resolve, Corrine forced a little smile, hoping he got her silent message and urgent plea. "You'll want to get started immediately. First we'll acquaint you with what we've been doing. You've got an all-day meeting with the mission specialists, whom I see you already know."

Frank and Jimmy beamed.

Mike never took his eyes off her, his big, leanly muscled body taut as wire. He said nothing.

"Then tomorrow, at 0800 hours, we'll get started on our SIM," she said, referring to their simulation in a huge tank of water that projected the approximate weightlessness of the environment in space. She was already wondering how she could get out of that exercise herself. "After training together for a week, becoming a team, we'll leave for Johnson Space Center, where we'll stay for the remaining months before launch, training on a daily basis."

He still just stared at her, his mouth grim, and in the depths of his fathomless eyes she saw things she didn't know how to respond to—surprise and shock, not to mention bitter disappointment at the way she'd handled this impossible situation.

Finally, after a long, hard moment in which she sweated buckets inside her far too stuffy suit, he slowly nodded, every inch of him serious and businesslike in a way that made her want to cry.

"See you then," he said, in a voice made of steel. Turning on his heel, he left the room, and Corrine could only watch him go.

And wonder at the odd sense of loss she experienced.

THE REST OF THE DAY was pure torture, and it was only day one. She had months left to go before she could be alone to lick her wounds and get over it.

Get over *what* exactly, Corrine wasn't sure, but she wasn't going to allow herself to think about it, not yet.

Not surprisingly, she ran into Mike twice more before the end of the day. Each time was more difficult than the last. The first was after his initial mission meeting. She happened to have the bad luck—which seemed to be following her around!—to be walking down the hallway as he came out of the conference room.

His shirtsleeves were shoved up; his hair was ruffled as if he'd run his fingers through it often. But his gaze went right to hers, and it was hot.

There were people everywhere, leaving her with no opportunity to do anything other than ask him about the meeting. He responded in kind, revealing nothing, for which she was grateful.

But as she walked away, quaking inside with so many unnamed emotions, she felt his gaze on her, and continued to feel it long after he was out of sight.

The second time she ran into him was in the middle of the night. The entire team was being housed on-site; each team member had a private bedroom, but they shared three community bathrooms.

Unfortunately for Corrine, she always seemed to need a pit stop around midnight, and this night was no exception. She left the bathroom and walked down the darkened hallway, plowing into a solid chest.

"Corrine."

There was no other voice in the world that could make her knees wobble. No other voice that could evoke so many thoughts and emotions that she quivered in response.

"We have to talk," he said.

"Not here." Panic such as she'd never known welled up in her, because with *this* man she felt weak. Vulnerable.

Not allowed.

She couldn't talk to him about their "problem," not yet, not until she had a better grip on her emotions and could fully control herself. He would *never* again see her without that control.

Memories flashed through her mind. She'd totally lost it with him, let him do anything and everything. She'd been spread-eagled and open on the hotel bed, with him kneeling over her, using his fingers, his tongue, his entire body to make her cry out and beg. That he'd cried out and begged, too, didn't matter. His control wasn't at question here, hers was.

"Talking won't help," she said. "It's done."

"It doesn't have to be."

What was he implying? That he wanted her

again? How was that possible, now that he knew who she was?

Didn't matter. She didn't want it to happen again. She wanted to move on, as if she'd never allowed her weakness, her loneliness, her momentary lapse of sanity to occur. "It's over, Mike." Saying his name helped. Her perfect stranger had a name and an identity to go along with that long, hard, warm body she'd worshipped all night long.

"Just like that?" he asked. "Fast as it started?"

"Yes."

"Harsh, don't you think?"

"That's life." She forced herself to remain cool when she had the most insane urge to ask for a hug. "Goodbye, Mike."

"You can't say goodbye to me. I'm on your team."

"I'm not saying goodbye to you as my teammate."

He shook his head and looked at her in a way that made her want to weep. "And I'm not saying goodbye to you as my lover—"

She set her finger on his lips, barely able to speak. "Don't say it," she begged. "Don't say anything."

He took her hand from his mouth and gently, so gently it brought up the tears she'd been fighting down, kissed her knuckles. "I won't," he said. "Only because I don't have to. We're not finished yet. And I think you know it."

Then he was gone.

5

AFTER THEIR middle of the night run-in, Mike slept poorly, haunted by visions of his new commander and her cool, cool eyes and even cooler voice.

Damn it, where had all that iciness come from? And why had she refused to acknowledge him and their night together, if only between them? Try as he might to make sense of it, he couldn't.

He understood the obvious. She was ashamed of what they'd shared. But why did that hurt?

As for how *he* felt, he was having a hard time reconciling the woman he'd held all night in his arms—the woman who'd showed him such passion and hunger—with the cool cucumber he'd been introduced to today.

Giving up on sleep, he got out of bed before dawn, still feeling insulted and angry, whether that was rational or not. With hours to spare before he had to be on site, he paced his room.

Damn it, he'd wanted this opportunity, had worked for it for years. He wouldn't let her ruin it.

He knew how he was going to spend the day—hell, probably the next week. He'd be in the water tank. It would be tedious, time consuming and restricting; they'd be in full scuba gear.

He couldn't wait, but first he had to get rid of some of this restless energy. He could hit the weight room or take a swim, but as he'd be spending every waking moment in the water for the foreseeable future, he decided to run.

Mike had left his room and was walking down the hall when Jimmy's head appeared outside his own door. Looking rumpled and tired, Jimmy took one look at Mike's running gear before he groaned. "Perfect. You're going to make us all look bad for the—" he glanced right, then left, then lowered his voice to a conspirator's whisper "—Ice Queen."

"Who?"

Frank stuck his head out another door, a fierce frown on his face. When he saw Mike and Jimmy, he grinned sleepily. "Hey, just like old times. You're going running? Wait for me—"

"*No,*" Jimmy said quickly, but Frank had already disappeared back into his room. Jimmy sighed. "Damn it, now I'll have to come, too, just to keep the two of you in line."

"Wait," Mike said. "About this Ice Queen thing—" But Jimmy had already shut the door in Mike's face.

He'd wanted to be alone, to burn off this undeniable, restless energy and to think, but he was destined for company now. Maybe that was for the better. Maybe he could stop thinking and just try to enjoy.

Frank and Jimmy were both dressed and ready to run within two minutes, and just as all three men started down the hallway together, yet another door opened.

Dressed in loose running shorts, a baggy tank top and aviator sunglasses that completely blocked her eyes from view, the commander herself emerged. She saw Jimmy and Frank first, both of whom happened to be standing in front of Mike, and she smiled. "Hey, guys. Up for some company?"

Then Mike stepped out from behind them. For lack of a better greeting, he lifted his hand and wagged his fingers at her.

Her expression froze. "Hello," she said flatly.

Hello. That was all she could manage. Not *I'm sorry I'm ignoring you*. Not *I didn't mean to deal you the biggest shock of your life*. Not *Wow, just the other night you made me come half a dozen times. Can you do it again?*

Instead she looked through him, as if only thirty hours ago he hadn't had her every which way but Sunday.

Frank hitched his head toward Mike. "We dragged his lazy butt out of bed, Commander. We're forcing him to run this morning so he can be in as good a shape as you."

Jimmy jumped right in. "He didn't want to come, ma'am. You should have heard all the new words he taught us, even though we asked him nicely."

Mike watched as good humor warred with wariness on Corrine's face. He still couldn't get used to knowing her real name, but it suited her. Just as the team suited her. Evidently, they'd gelled as a group during their time together. Their camaraderie bode well for the mission.

It didn't bode well for him. For one, he hated being the outsider. He didn't mind the work entailed to catch up; in fact he would thrive on the challenge of it. But damn it, he wanted her to like him, not look at him as if he were some sort of deviant.

He didn't understand how she could go from soft, laughing and full of heat to hard as nails, unsmiling and totally controlled.

Oh, and then there was the kicker—she was his commander. He'd seen her naked, sprawled out beneath him and whimpering for more, and she was his damn boss.

"Let's go," he said as lightly as he could. "Let's see who keeps up with who. And just so you know," he added to Frank and Jimmy, "I plan on outrunning both of you."

His friends simply exchanged knowing smiles. Which only doubled Mike's determination.

They started off at a quick pace. Not that Mike couldn't easily maintain it, but he remembered Jimmy and Frank·as not being the most disciplined of men. Curiously enough, they were disciplined now.

Corrine stayed with them, silent and determined, and he wondered how long she could hold her own. Wondered, too, how she would give in. Would she gracefully drop back, or kill herself trying to keep up? He told himself he didn't care. Either way, it would give him great pleasure to see her sweat.

At the twenty-minute mark no one had even slowed, but Mike was starting to sweat. Jimmy and Frank, too, especially since they'd kept up a steady stream of banter all along about the exploits they'd shared with Mike in Russia.

"You should have seen the crowd after we landed in '97," Frank said to Corrine, who might or might not have been listening, as she never slowed her pace or glanced over. "The Russian women couldn't get enough of Mike. He's a huge celebrity. They yell and cry for him as if he were Mel Gibson."

Jimmy snorted. "Yeah, tough job we had, fighting them off for him. And then there was that one who sneaked into his shower in the hotel room. Remember, Frank? Remember how he screamed like a pansy?"

"She scared the hell out of me," Mike said in his own defense, sending a sheepish glance at Corrine.

She didn't so much as crack a smile.

"Oh, you poor baby," Jimmy said, now gasping for air. "Hey, can you still get a different woman every night if you want?"

"Uh..." Another glance at Corrine assured him she was listening, after all; her face had definitely gone a shade redder. What he didn't know was whether she was exhibiting embarrassment or anger. "I never had a different woman every night."

"Right. You took Sundays off."

Definitely anger, Mike decided, as Corrine's face darkened even more.

Frank and Jimmy took great delight in his growing discomfort, but they had no way of knowing they were innocently revealing parts of him he absolutely, positively didn't want exposed in front of this woman.

Apparently he hadn't yet made the switch from Corrine's lover to her teammate. He was going to have to do that sooner or later.

At the forty-minute mark, he started huffing, but refused to show it, distracting himself by watching the commander's tush swing gently to and fro with each stride.

The clothes she wore were a crime, he decided. She had an incredible body, lush and curvy in all the good spots, tough as nails in others. He knew this, as he'd personally kissed and sucked and stroked every single inch of her.

But both yesterday in her stern suit, and now in the loose jogging clothes, she hid it all.

That alone was going to kill him, if not the pace. And then suddenly, mercifully, both Frank and Jimmy slowed to a walk, waving them on.

Mike glanced at Corrine, more than ready to let her concede defeat, because there was no mistake to be made here, this was some sort of pissing contest, and he intended to win.

She never even glanced at him, just stared straight ahead, her legs and arms pumping for all she was worth. And she'd hardly broken a sweat.

"Tired?" he asked as casually as he could while sucking serious wind. "Because we could slow down."

"Feel free," she said, and actually picked up speed, starting to leave him in her dust.

Holy shit, was all he could think, kicking into as high a gear as she had.

She was going to kill him.

"Please don't continue for my sake." She actually had the nerve to toss that over her shoulder in an even, controlled voice that only fueled his frustration.

He could hardly breathe, much less answer. "I'm fine," he said through his teeth.

"Suit yourself."

They went another mile in silence while he stewed over the fact that at the hotel he'd suggested she rest while climbing a damn flight of stairs.

After a while, she shot him a glance. "Oh for God's sake, Mike. Stop, would you?"

"No."

"You're just being stubborn."

True, but damned if he was going to admit it.

"What if I ordered you to stop?"

"You can't do that."

"Why not?" She shoved up her glasses to rest on top of her head, and her clear, midnight blue eyes stared right at him.

That he could remember when they were cloudy and opaque with lust really ticked him off.

"You can't order me to do anything," he said. Or rather, gasped. "We're not working at the moment."

Her jaw tightened, but she didn't break stride. "I should have known. You're going to be a male chauvinist pig about this."

"What?"

"You can't work for a woman, right?"

"Ha!" he gasped, but then had to go quiet to concentrate on getting oxygen to his poor body. "I can work for a woman. And—" And he was fresh out of air. "I'm...not...a...pig."

"Male *chauvinist* pig."

Okay, now she was *trying* to rile him, but before he could accuse her of that, she slowed, then finally stopped. Ignoring him, she went about a series of stretches to cool down, while Mike just concentrated on staying conscious.

He found himself watching her as she spread her legs, then bent over, her palms flat on the ground.

For just a moment, her shorts tightened across her tight, curvy butt and his hands actually itched to touch.

How was it that he hadn't noticed what incredible shape she was in? He couldn't believe it, but she was actually in better shape than he was, and he was pretty damn fit.

"Look," she said, suddenly straightening and looking him right in the eye, somehow managing to stare down her nose at him at the same time, even though she was nearly a foot shorter than he. "I can see you're going to have problems working under me, but get over it. You're our third and last choice. There is no one else. I won't compromise the mission."

He didn't know whether to be flattered or insulted, so he brilliantly stood there like an idiot.

"Your reputation precedes you," she continued, blowing a strand of hair out of her face that dared defy its confines. "Both in and out of the space shuttle. I'm well aware of your profile, but I didn't expect to have problems so soon."

He blinked and straightened, breathing trouble and screaming muscles forgotten. "Excuse me? *Problems?*"

She just looked at him.

"Are you referring to the fact that we've been naked together?" he asked bluntly.

That chin of hers thrust even higher into the air, and she pointed at him. "And I want you to stop that."

"Stop what, exactly?"

"Referring to…you know."

"Being naked?" he asked, feeling wicked and angry, which didn't make a very good combination. "Or having sex?"

She whirled and walked away.

Because she was moving along at a good clip,

and because he couldn't walk without whimpering, he let her go.

But they still weren't finished, not by a long shot.

THE TEAM SPENT THE DAY in the water simulator, working some of the experiments they'd be taking up with them. Although heavy equipment was weightless in space, it still wasn't easy to move around.

Corrine knew the general public had no idea how strong an astronaut had to be. To relocate a large mass, which described all of their equipment, you had to apply a large force, taking care to exert it precisely or the object would twist and turn uncontrollably. An equally large, well-directed, controlled force was required to stop any motion.

In other words, brute strength.

Even something as simple as trying to screw a bolt into a piece of equipment required finesse. That sort of maneuver couldn't be done while floating in the cabin. Anchors were needed, or footholds, in order to apply force, which required special techniques, special tools, special processes, and often the coordinated efforts of a teammate. Everything, even the easiest of tasks, had to be practiced over and over and over again.

One of the biggest challenges they faced was that a true space environment couldn't be simulated exactly on earth. Hence the "SIMs" in large bodies of water, with astronauts in scuba gear. It was the closest they could come to the real experience, even with today's vast technological advances.

Corrine climbed into bed that night, thinking things had gone well. That is, if she discounted the dark, questioning looks she'd gotten at every turn from her pilot, Mike Wright.

She still couldn't believe her rotten luck. How was it that she couldn't even manage to have an anonymous affair?

If Mike had his way, it wouldn't be anonymous at all! She couldn't have that, absolutely could not let the others on the team know what she'd done with him in a moment of selfish weakness.

And what she'd done was still interrupting her sleep. She couldn't close her eyes without feeling his body brush hers, without remembering how he tasted, or the incredibly sexy sounds he made when he—

She flopped over in bed yet again and stared at

the ceiling, but an almost unbearable sense of loneliness came over her. Why now? This was the life she'd willingly chosen. She'd known it would be a dog-eat-dog world, that she'd be forgoing any indulgence of her femininity to make it. She'd known that, had even craved it—she who'd never quite mastered being...well, a woman. So what was this sudden longing to be just that, to let someone in, to be vulnerable, soft? Giving. Even loving.

With Mike.

Wow, that thought came from nowhere and extinguished any amount of sleepiness she might have mustered. She flipped over again, but the damage had been done, Mike was back in her mind. And all she could think of was how he'd looked coming out of the water simulator earlier, when he'd stripped out of his cumbersome gear down to nothing but a pair of wet, clingy swimming trunks.

Sleek, wet and muscular, that had been Mike, standing there on deck.

She'd taken one look at him and had lost every thought in her head. He'd known it, too, damn him; she could still see the slow, baby-here-I-am smile he'd sent her.

This had to stop. She'd had him once and that should be enough. It should be over.

But it wasn't.

She couldn't even look at him without having that stupid, adolescent, weak-kneed reaction, and it was really making her furious.

She'd read his personnel files, shamelessly soaking up his private information. He had four brothers, all in the military. His father, too, was a military man. His mother, a Russian, had died when Mike had been only four, so it was no wonder he was so incredibly masculine. He'd grown up in a house full of Y chromosomes, and then had gone into an industry overloaded with testosterone.

That was a problem, she decided, rolling over to punch her pillow. Because while Mike definitely knew how to treat a woman—he had, after all, made her purr more than once—he had no idea how to do anything other than pamper a female, much less work for one. To work beneath her command was going to be utterly foreign to him, and with both of them needing their control…well, it wasn't going to go smoothly, this mission, she could see that.

What she couldn't see, exactly, was what to do about it.

She wasn't herself around him. She had a hard time sticking to that cool, icy facade she favored, mostly because he saw right through her.

She hated that.

With a sigh, she heaved herself out of bed for her usual middle of the night run to the bathroom. It was annoying, but then again, if she'd just sleep the night through like normal people, instead of obsessing, she wouldn't have to go at all, would she?

The hall was silent, both when she crept into the bathroom and when she came out two minutes later. Which was why she nearly screamed when she ran into a solid rock wall of a chest.

Even as those big, warm hands came up to steady her, she knew. "Mike," she said in a breathless whisper, blinking through the dark.

"Fancy meeting you here."

"You have a weak bladder, too?"

"I don't have a weak anything."

"Everyone has a weak something."

"What I have," he said softly, reaching up to tug on her ponytail, "is a weakness for long dark hair flowing wild and free, and dark-blue eyes melting with desire when they look at me, instead of two icicles."

"I'm going back to bed."

"Not until we talk."

"It's late."

He flicked the light on his watch. "Actually, it's early. I've been listening for you, Corrine. We need to get this over with."

"Maybe you'd rather try to beat me at my morning run again."

He scowled. "So I underestimated you."

"You thought me nothing more than a fragile doll."

"This isn't what I wanted to talk about."

"I bet. Look, Mike, this is never going to work. Surely you can see that. You have a problem with me being the commander of this mission."

"What I have a problem with is you pretending you don't know me. You pretending we didn't sleep together, that we didn't make love—"

She slapped his hand over his mouth and whipped her head to the right, then to the left, making sure no one could hear them. "Damn it," she breathed. "Could you stop talking about it? Why do we have to keep talking about it?"

Grabbing her hands away from his mouth, he held them at her sides, slowly backing her up against the wall until she had the cool plaster at her back and his hot, hot body at her front.

She hadn't given much thought to her pajamas—men's flannel shorts and a loose tank top. As they were her favorites, they'd been washed to a thin softness. Thin enough to feel every inch of him, and her body seemed to recognize how much she'd enjoyed those inches, because she closed her eyes in order to better concentrate on the sensations.

"Corrine," he whispered, his voice low and rough now, as if he, too, couldn't help himself. "I don't understand you. Help me understand. Why can't we just…be? Why do we have to ignore this?"

Why? He had to ask why? There were a million reasons, starting with the fact that they had to work together professionally, with no personal hangups between them. The mission depended on it. NASA counted on it. Billions of tax dollars were at stake. There could be nothing dragging them down emotionally. "There is no 'this,'" she said with a finality she didn't feel.

He ran a finger over her jaw, down her throat

to the base of her neck, where her pulse had taken off. "Liar," he chided softly as her nipples beaded and thrust against the material of her shirt.

"Mike."

"Yeah."

She let out a disparaging sound. *Oh, Mike.* Why couldn't she forget? What was it about what they'd shared in the dark, dark of the night with no music and no candles, no romantic devices, nothing but the two of them turning to each other? They'd needed nothing but each other, and that scared her.

Hell, it terrified her. "There *can't* be a this," she whispered.

"Oh, there's a this." His finger continued its path over her collarbone to her shoulder, nudging the edge of the tank off it. Stepping even closer, he dipped his head and nipped at the skin he'd exposed, while his fingers continued their seductive assault on her senses.

Thunk. The back of her head hit the wall as she lost the ability to hold it up. "Mike—"

"How can you ignore me?" He dipped his head so that she could feel his breath on her skin. "After what we shared?"

"It was…just…sex," she panted as he dragged

that clever mouth back up her throat now, feasting as he went, his fingers toying with the edging of her top, and the curve of her breast.

"Yeah. Sex. Great sex." He waited until she cleared her glassy gaze and looked at him. "I made you come, remember?" His hips slid to hers. "Over and over, until you were screaming."

She was going to scream now. "Stop." Since she wanted to mean it, she put a hand to his chest. "I want you to forget all that. If we're going to make this work, you have to forget."

"Corrine—"

"*Forget*, Mike." And while she still had the strength, she wrenched away. But instead of going back to bed, she went into the bathroom and cranked on the shower.

Cold.

As she stripped and stepped beneath the icy spray, she could swear she heard Mike's soft, mocking laughter.

6

THE MEETING WAS NOT going well. Corrine knew this, and she tried to get a handle on things— things being mostly her own emotions. But with Mike sitting there so calm and put together at the conference table, it was all but impossible.

She could feel his eyes on her, searching and intense. And though it had to be only an illusion, she thought she could smell him, all clean, sexy male. She certainly could feel him, and he wasn't even touching her.

She'd dreamed about that, his touching her. He did it far too often. Always in such a way as to seem innocent, of course. A brush of an arm here. A thigh there. Here a touch, there a touch, everywhere a touch.

She was losing it.

"Facts are facts," she said into the tense silence. "We've been asked to conduct these experiments, and we will."

"But we can complain about it, at least. They're not NASA based, or even university experiments," Frank said. They'd been having this bickering session for an hour. "It's a bunch of elementary students from Missouri, and they want to test *seeds*. I think we can all agree that, with the unknown time factor involved in repairing the already installed solar panels, combined with constructing the new ones, we have better things to be worrying about than kids with seeds."

Both Jimmy and Stephen nodded. Corrine looked at Mike.

He returned the look, his expression closed, and said nothing.

"I hear what you're saying," she said, a bit unsettled by how that simple exchange could rattle her wits. "But these kids—middle school, not elementary—won a national contest in D.C. It was a publicity stunt, designed to bring the public's attention back to the space shuttle and the International Space Station in a positive way." That she personally agreed with her team—that they had far better uses for their very limited time in space—didn't matter. Her hands were tied. She had no choice. "We have to do this. The president promised we would."

"Commander, surely he could—"

She shook her head at Jimmy, hating that she couldn't find her cool, purposeful calm with Mike sitting there watching her. This should be easy, persuading her team to do whatever she wanted them to do. She shouldn't feel their bitter disappointment in her inability to change the unchangeable. "The president personally asked NASA for this favor, and we agreed."

"Yes, but when we agreed," Stephen pointed out, clearly annoyed, "it was *before* we knew about the additional time problems we were going to face, both in transport and on the station."

As the payload specialist, he had viable concerns regarding the time constraints. Corrine knew this, which didn't make her tough stance any easier. The International Space Station, or ISS, had had its share of problems, the current and biggest being the defective solar panels already in place. Since astronauts were housed on the ISS on a permanent basis, repairing the problem was crucial.

No one wanted to spend critical hours every day of their ten-day flight baby-sitting the students' projects, which included exposing seeds, hair, bread, hamburger and even bubble gum to the weightless environment of space to see if they were affected by the change in pressure, altitude or anything else.

"We still hadn't figured out how to add the required replacement parts to our payload without crushing the original load," Jimmy said. "Much less allow time for the repairs Stephen has to perform." He lifted a troubled gaze to both Corrine and Mike, who as commander and pilot, together would run the ship. "We're running out of time."

"Not to mention, maneuvering into the tight area of the ISS is going to take a miracle," Frank added. "Are you prepared for that? Prepared to tell the other countries in this mess with us that we couldn't figure it all out because we were too busy handling amateur science experiments?"

"You don't understand the pressure NASA is under to have the public on side in this huge tax expense," Corrine said evenly. "The microgravity of space has become an important tool for developing new and sophisticated materials." She purposely didn't look at Mike, so she could let her famed iciness fill her voice. She was in charge here and had the final say, whether they liked it or not. "And the public is losing interest."

"Good," Stephen said, and both Jimmy and Frank laughed.

"Not good," Corrine corrected. "We need a total of forty-three flights to build the ISS. That's quite a bit of taxpayer money."

"We're already committed as a nation," Stephen said. "It's too late for them to decide they don't want in. I'm with Frank and Jimmy. Dump the experiments."

"Stephen," Mike said softly. "This isn't a democracy."

Corrine took a deep breath but didn't look at Mike. He was siding with her, apparently. Because he agreed, or because she'd slept with him? She hated that she questioned it. "We're not ditching the experiments."

Stephen's jaw tightened.

Jimmy looked irritated, too, but asked calmly, "Can we agree to shelve them if we have a problem up there?"

"We'll make that decision when and if the time comes," Corrine said.

"Well, let's work on the timetable then," Stephen said, still grumbling. In a low mutter he added, "And make sure nothing conflicts, especially a PMS schedule. Geez."

The rest of the men appeared to fight for control of their facial expressions, and lost. Jimmy and Frank grinned.

Mike wisely looked down at his clamped hands.

But Corrine was infuriated, anyway. Why was it if a woman had a strong opinion, or needed to get her group under control, she came off as a moody bitch? But when a man did so, he was merely acting within his rights as a male in charge?

The unfairness wasn't new to Corrine, but for some reason, today it hit hard. She chalked it up to a lack of sleep, *not* the unquenched heat Mike had kindled within her body last night, and used her don't-mess-with-me expression to stare down the men.

Jimmy and Frank were unhappy, to say the least. Stephen looked equally so. "I think this stinks," he said. "For the record."

"It doesn't matter what you think," Mike said evenly.

Fair or not, at his defense of her, Corrine felt smoke come out of her ears. She didn't want any heroics here, she wanted…she wanted—Oh hell. She wanted *him*, damn it! "Obviously we need a break," she said, standing. "Now's a good a time as any."

Mike was the last to the door, and she stopped him. "I want to talk to you."

"Do you?"

"I don't need defending." She knew she sounded stiff and ungrateful, but as she was both at the moment, she couldn't help it. "Especially in front of my team. Not now, not ever."

"It's my team, too," he said softly. Too softly. "And I won't let anyone talk to you like that. Not now, not ever," he said, mocking her words, while somehow utterly meaning what he'd said.

If she'd had more sleep, she would have seen it coming and deflected it. But as it was, she'd been sidetracked by all that heat in his gaze, so that when he cupped her cheek and stroked her jaw with his big, warm and oddly tender hand, all she could do was stand there and tremble like a damn virgin.

"Corrine."

"No," she whispered.

"You don't even know what I was going to say."

"I don't want to know."

"I'm going to tell you anyway."

"Please, don't."

"Please." His lips curved. "The only time I've ever heard you say that word was when I was buried inside you and—"

"Mike!"

His eyes darkened. "And that, too. The way you say my name. Makes me hard, Corrine."

"I'll be sure never to say it again," she said through her teeth.

"I want you." He shook his head, clearly baffled. "God, I still want you."

She crossed her arms, desperately striving for normalcy, which was impossible with this man. He set her body humming without even trying. "We were talking about what happened in this room a few minutes ago. About the fact that you came to my defense when I didn't need it."

"No, *you* were talking about that. *I* wanted to talk about something entirely different. Or not talk." His eyes flared with an unmistakable desire. "Not talk is okay, too."

This was far worse than she could have believed, because how could all this...this *heat* still be between them? They'd had each other, more than once! It should be over.

Done.

And where had her anger gone? How was it that whenever she so much as looked at him, she lost every thought in her head? And how in the hell was she going to keep it to herself?

"So many worries," he said quietly, holding her face while he forced her to look into his eyes. "Share them with me."

"Yeah, right," she managed to answer weakly, pushing away his hands. "I can't."

"Won't you mean." He watched her pace the room. "Why are you doing this? Why are you this warm, soft, passionate woman with me, and yet with your team you're so…"

She whirled on him. "So what?"

"Hard," he said bluntly. "You're hard, Cor-rine."

That hurt, and she had to swallow before she could talk. "If I have to explain it to you, you'll never understand."

"Try."

She looked into his earnest face and for some odd reason felt her throat tighten. "Mike. Not here."

By some mercy, footsteps came down the hall.

"Later then," he agreed. "But, Corrine? There *will* be a later."

AT LEAST THE AFTERNOON session went more smoothly, though the damage had been done. Corrine was as uptight as she could possibly be.

Everyone else seemed willing to move on from the morning's scene, however, so she put all her remaining tension behind a cool smile and a hard determination.

After all, she had work to do and a mission to whip into shape. The solar array wings they'd be carting into space had to be treated with kid gloves, both while packing and transporting, and then while constructing and assembling on the space station.

Each of the mission members, Corrine, Mike, Stephen, Frank and Jimmy, had a specific job, and each job was critical, requiring months and months of planning, and then months and months more of actual, hands-on practice. For instance, while attaching the very large solar array wings, each of which, when fully deployed, would stretch two hundred forty feet from wingtip to wingtip, Corrine first had to maneuver the shuttle into position so that they could open the payload bay and work in there. That alone—shifting a space shuttle in the available window at the ISS—would be an amazing feat.

Stephen and Mike would operate the robotic arm. Frank and Jimmy, both of whom had extensive technical training, would do the actual repair. Three space walks were required, and each time, the robotic arm would be used as a movable platform for an astronaut to lie on. That astronaut, Jimmy in this case, would be strapped in, with Corrine directing Mike and Stephen into maneuvering Jimmy where he needed to go. The integrated equipment assembly measured sixteen by sixteen by sixteen feet, and weighed twelve thousand pounds. It required very precise teamwork, all done in a weightless atmosphere, hovering between the tight corridor of the space shuttle and the ISS, while wearing a bulky, hundred-pound spacesuit.

Mind-boggling, when she allowed herself to think about it. She and the others would literally have their lives in each other's hands.

Practice. Definitely practice.

As pilot, Mike spent much of the day right by her side. They weren't alone, not even for a second. Though every inch of skin was literally hidden from view—everything but their eyes, through the viewing lens on their mask—she was so aware of him that every time he so much as drew in a deep breath, she knew it. If he looked at her, she felt it.

And when he accidentally—or maybe not so accidentally—brushed up against her, her senses went into overdrive.

She didn't like it.

She ignored it.

She did so by remaining cool and in control, refusing to be baited or sidetracked. Once, when the rest of the team was on the other side of the large mechanism they were using to hoist the huge pieces of equipment, Mike planted himself in front of her, purposely looking directly into her mask as his gloved hands slipped to her hips and gently but deliberately squeezed.

They were separated by layers and layers, and yet she felt his fingers as if they were skin to skin. Her eyes fluttered closed, her heart picked up speed. And she actually ached. *Ached.*

When she forced her eyes open, she expected triumph to flare in his own deep, dark-brown gaze, but all she saw was his own response, which mirrored hers.

After that, it got harder and harder to ignore him. As a result, maybe she worked them all a little harder than she might have, but she told herself she was a perfectionist and simply expected the best out of them.

That they were delivering that best went a long way toward easing the knowledge that the rest of the team didn't especially like her. But they respected her, and had the same work ethic she did, so that would have to be good enough.

Besides, she was used to not being liked. Not many understood her drive, her need to succeed. At times, she didn't understand it herself. Her parents supported her; her friends supported her. All her life she'd been loved and cherished. It wasn't a lack in any of those things that drove her but a simple, overriding hunger for success.

And she would have it.

MIKE WAITED IN THE DARK, in the hallway, silent and tense and listening for Corrine's standard midnight run to the bathroom.

It was stupid, even pathetic, especially when he had no idea what he wanted to say or do.

Actually, that was one big, fat lie.

He knew *exactly* what he wanted to do to her, and it involved no clothes, a bed and lots of moaning.

What was this crazy need he had for her? It

made no sense. Especially when she'd made it clear she wanted to forget she'd ever known him. He should want to forget her, too, given what a tough, no-nonsense commander she was.

But he couldn't forget. And so he waited.

She didn't disappoint. Just past midnight, she came out of her room, wearing her men's boxers and tank top.

Shrinking back into the shadows, he watched her as she walked with her frank, here-I-come gait until she disappeared into the bathroom.

When she came back out, yawning broadly, he grabbed her.

She nearly screamed, but quickly controlled herself. And while he admired her control on the job, he didn't want her in control now, he wanted her hot and bothered and unsettled, which happened to be the only time he got to see the woman he suspected was the real Corrine Atkinson.

She fought him, but he used his superior strength to haul her closer until they were chest to chest, thigh to thigh, and all the delicious spots in the middle were meshed together.

Ah, just what the doctor ordered.

"What are you doing?" she whispered fiercely.

Hell if he knew. "How about this?" And he captured her mouth with his.

Immediately she went utterly, completely still, and he knew he had her. If she'd fought him, he'd have let her go instantly. If she'd given him any sign that this wasn't where she wanted to be, he'd have stepped back and gone to bed. He might have been hard as steel and frustrated beyond belief, but he would have gone.

She didn't give him that sign, but she didn't kiss him back, either. He wanted so much more, wanted to see her eyes slumberous and sexy with the same hunger he felt, wanted her body humming and needy for his, wanted her to look at him the way she had in his hotel room, the look that told him he was the only one who could possibly do it for her in that moment.

He thought maybe he wanted even more, but that idea unsettled him, so he concentrated on the physical craving instead. Her mouth was warm and tasted exactly as he remembered. Gentling his hold, he smoothed his hands up and down her back while nibbling at her lips, teasing as he sought the entrance she would have to willingly give him.

It wasn't until he said her name softly, cupping

her face so that he could look deep into her eyes, that she let out a quiet hum and slid her arms around his neck. "Mike."

He let out a rough groan when she tilted her head, searching for a deeper connection. And he gave it to her. Within two seconds that connection was not only deeper but scorchingly hot. Corrine had one hand fisted in his hair, holding him tight as if she thought he might back away.

Fat chance.

Her other hand slid around his waist, her fingers slipping beneath his T-shirt to the base of his spine before stroking up his bare back. A simple touch, even an innocent one, but it set him on fire. His hands were busy, too, dancing down her arms to her hips, sliding beneath her shirt to glide along bare, warm skin he couldn't get enough of. Their kiss was long, wet, deep and noisy, but just as he brought his hands around to cup her breasts, one of the bedroom doors behind them opened.

Corrine froze and he felt her horror. Silently swearing at the loss of her hot body and their privacy, he put a finger to her lips and quickly backed her into the bathroom.

Like two teenagers they stood stock-still in the dark room, listening.

Nothing.

"My God," she whispered. "I can't believe I— That you— That we—"

"Nearly ate each other up?"

"Don't say it."

She sounded disgusted, and it made him mad at her all over again. Why, he wondered, did he care about this woman? Why did he care that his teammates were grumbling about her cool and controlled demeanor, that they didn't see the real Corrine as he did? Why did he care that beyond the facade she showed the world, she had the deepest, most soul-wrenching eyes he'd ever seen?

"We nearly...*again.*" She closed her eyes and rubbed her temples, and her abject misery fueled his growing temper.

"You can only have sex with me as a stranger? Is that it?"

"We were not having sex!"

"So when you were writhing and panting in my arms only a minute ago, tearing at my shirt, whimpering for more, pawing at me, demanding more...what was that?"

She tried to stare him down, but he didn't stare down easily. He could see the wheels turning in her head as she strove for a way to make this okay in her little dream world, where they didn't have this shocking need for each other.

"All we did just now was kiss," she said finally, nodding her head as if she could live with that particular fantasy.

Time to pop her little bubble.

"Honey," he said with a disbelieving laugh, "if that was just a kiss, I'll eat my shorts."

"It was!"

"How is it then that you were two seconds from coming, and I'd barely even touched your breasts?"

He didn't need light to see the hot flush of anger on her face. "You're impossible!" she spat. "I really hate that!"

"And you're ashamed of what we did. I hate that."

They stared at each other, but there was nothing left to say.

7

THE NEXT DAY WAS SPENT in one meeting after another again, and by the end of it, Corrine was mentally drained.

It wasn't the work; she loved that. It was Mike.

She couldn't forget how he'd looked when he told her he thought she was ashamed of what they'd done.

She'd let him believe it, and in doing so, had hurt him.

See? *This* was what happened when one acted irresponsibly. And having sex with a stranger in his hotel room definitely constituted an irresponsible act.

But it was the oddest thing...she couldn't truly bring herself to regret what they'd done. Not one moment of it. She sure as hell wasn't ashamed, either. Which meant, for honesty's sake, she had to set the record straight. Then and only then could she get on with life and put her full concentration into this mission.

It took a while until she was free of the bureaucracy and red tape she had to dance through all day in her meetings with NASA officials, scientists from no less than five other countries, and a representative for the students' experiments, but finally she went in search of Mike. Her intention was to straighten this out, which in no way explained why her body was humming at just the thought of seeing him again. Nope, she attributed that to hunger.

She couldn't find him. She couldn't find any of her team. As a last resort, she hunted down Ed, one of the administrative assistants.

"They're out to dinner," he said.

"They?"

"Your team."

Was that pity in his eyes? It was hard to tell, as he vanished as soon as he'd answered, reminding her that most of the assistants lived in terror of her.

For no real reason, she told herself. Yes, she was usually in a hurry. And maybe sometimes she could be...well, abrupt. It wasn't anything personal, though.

But her team going off without her, now *that*, she was pretty certain, was personal.

No biggie. She didn't want to eat with them, anyway.

Much. Besides, she had work to do.

She stayed late to prove it, but she knew damn well a small part of her was wondering if any of them would come back after dinner to see how she was doing.

Ah, geez. Pathetic. She hated that she'd been reduced to thinking such nonsense.

Get over it and move on.

THAT NIGHT SHE LAY AWAKE, staring at the ceiling. The mission was far from her mind, which was otherwise occupied by a tall, leanly muscled, beautiful man who, when he smiled could talk her into jumping off a cliff.

Maybe he'd be waiting to pounce on her in the hallway, she thought at midnight, leaping to her feet, her heart racing in anticipation. But as she made her way to the bathroom, as slowly and loudly as she dared, no one grabbed her. Not then, and not when she came out.

She was alone, truly alone, just as she'd always wanted to be.

BEFORE HE KNEW IT, their week at Marshall Space Flight Center was over. Mike and the rest of the team were leaving for Houston and the Johnson Space Center, where they would remain in training until mission launch at Kennedy Space Center, Florida.

There was much left to be done. At Johnson Space Center, each of them would be run through their paces. Over and over again. Loading. Unloading. Constructing. Repairing. Reconstructing. Takeoff. Landing. Going through each possible scenario, and just when they thought they were close to done, they'd be ordered to do it again.

NASA took it all very seriously. Having had painful, painful failures in the past, mistakes that had cost billions, not to mention the taxpayers faith, they didn't care to repeat any of those mistakes.

Mike understood this all too well, and still he loved his job. He loved everything except the fact he was working for a woman he wanted to kiss stupid, and he couldn't quite get that out of his head.

He planned to travel to Houston the way he'd traveled to Huntsville, piloting himself in his honey of a plane, which he'd rebuilt himself.

Frank had also flown himself into Marshall, so he flew himself out. But Stephen and Jimmy jumped at Mike's offer to come along with him.

And to his shock, so did Corrine.

She appeared on the tarmac, her bag on her shoulder. "You have room for one more?"

"Absolutely." At the sudden, awkward silence, Mike glanced at Stephen and Jimmy, both of whom shrugged noncommittally. Their faces had been wiped clear of the laughter they'd just been sharing over some obscene joke, but even *they* were professional enough not to quibble if their commander wanted to horn in on their ride.

With Stephen and Jimmy preoccupied admiring Mike's work on the Lear, Corrine moved close. "I wanted to talk to you."

"You've said that before." Mike lifted a brow. "And haven't really meant it."

Shifting from one foot to the other, she let out a half laugh, and he realized with some shock that she was nervous. Corrine never looked nervous, and his curiosity twitched. She seemed so put together in her business suit, revealing none of her lush curves and warm softness. He remembered both so well that her armor didn't matter, and his curiosity wasn't the only thing that twitched.

Damn her anyway, for standing there killing him, for being so heart-wrenchingly beautiful. "Talk away then," he said with far more lightness than he felt.

"Okay, good. Thanks." She set down her bag. "You've been avoiding me."

Yes, he had. Self-preservation. But damned if he was going to tell her that. Mike Wright avoided no one. "How is that possible? We've been working side by side for over a week now."

A breeze blew over them, but Corrine had her hair tightly back and beaten into submission. Not a strand moved, not as it had that night they'd been together, when her mane of hair had flowed over his hot flesh, teasing him with its silky scent.

"Yes, we worked together," she agreed. "But we haven't…"

It was wrong to pretend he had no idea what she was trying to say—wrong, but ever so satisfying. "Yes?" he coaxed. "We haven't…?"

She let out a huff of breath. "You know. Talked. Or…"

Even more satisfying was her blush. "Are you referring to our hot, wet, long kisses? Or the hot, wet fun we had in my hotel room?"

Her eyes darkened. Her mouth turned grim.

"It was a mistake to bring this up. I'm sorry." She went to step past him and into the plane, but he stopped her.

"It was wrong," he said in a harsh whisper. "Because you don't really want to talk about it. You want to forget it ever happened. You're ashamed—"

"No." She put a hand to his chest, deflating his sudden anger with just one touch. "I'm not ashamed. That's what I wanted to tell you. I'm sorry I let you think it."

For a moment, she actually let him see inside her, past the aloofness and into the woman he'd held so closely that night. It gave him a funny ache in his chest. "Why do you do that?" he whispered, unable to help himself from stroking her arm. "Why do you let them think of you as the Ice Queen? I know you're not."

Her eyes widened; her mouth opened, then carefully shut. "What?"

His stomach fell. "Nothing." God, she didn't know what they called her. "Nothing at all."

"What?" she finally said again, very, very softly. "What did you say they call me?"

His fault, that devastating, stricken look in her eyes, and though she managed to hide it with amazing speed and grace, he couldn't have felt worse. "Corrine—"

"Never mind." She straightened her shoulders, lifted her chin high. "No need for me to be insulted when it's the truth."

"Wait…"

"No, let's not. We have a meeting this afternoon and need to hustle."

"Yes, but—"

"You going to fly this baby or what?" she snapped, stepping aboard. She nodded curtly to the others, without an outward sign that she'd just been brought to her knees.

"Final inspection complete?" she asked Mike when he slid into the pilot's seat.

"Done. Corrine—"

"Don't." Sitting there next to him in the cockpit, as if she belonged there, she proceeded to grab his clipboard and start the preflight check.

He grabbed it back. "I've got it."

She picked up his headphones and would have put them on, but in *his* plane, *he* was in charge. He took those from her as well.

"Route?" She ran her hands over the controls.

"I know how to get us there." He brushed her fingers away from the instrument panel.

She shot him a look of annoyance. "Then do it."

He ignored the tone of that remark, because he understood she was hurt. But with her obnoxious, controlling attitude, he was damn close to forgetting how lush and warm and giving she could be.

He didn't like it.

In fact, he downright hated that aloofness, and decided to destroy it. He waited until they were in the air and Corrine was fully relaxed, lost in her own little world. Perfect. She was reading an aviation magazine, deeply engrossed, when he reached over and put his hand on her thigh.

She nearly leaped out of her skin.

Oh yeah, he thought, wisely keeping his grin to himself, his good humor restored. He'd gone at this thing all wrong. Letting her build up her defenses wasn't the answer; driving her crazy was, and apparently he could do that with just a touch.

"Could you hand me a tissue?" he asked, gesturing toward the small box next to her right hip. Before he removed his hand from her thigh, he stroked her, just once.

She fumbled and dropped the tissue, then

jerked when she finally handed it to him and their fingers touched.

He smiled, and her gaze went to his mouth.

Bingo, he thought, pleased with himself. Very pleased. For the rest of the flight he touched her whenever possible, when no one else would see. He even managed to suck on her earlobe for one delicious second.

She nearly leaped out of her skin then, too, but she didn't say a word. Just glared at him while the flush on her cheeks and her shallow breathing gave her away.

He expected great satisfaction to course through him, as he'd indeed shattered her aloofness, but since she was clearly furious at him for doing so, it was somehow a hollow victory.

IN HOUSTON, things were different. Everyone on the team but Mike lived there, so they had their own home to go to every night. NASA had booked a hotel suite for Mike, so there were no more clandestine, late-night bathroom "meetings" in the barracks.

Corrine missed them.

A week into their training at Johnson Space Center, she knew she had a problem. It wasn't the team; they were working well together. More than well, mostly because now that she knew they thought of her as the Ice Queen, she used it to her advantage. She wasn't there to make friends, she told herself, but to lead a team.

Once again, the problem was Mike.

He was driving her crazy. Yes, he'd kept their secret; he hadn't told a soul about their wild night of passion. But he was no longer ignoring her. Well, that wasn't true. To anyone else, anyone who didn't know of their past, Mike and Corrine were working together. Period. They'd see nothing but a professional link as the two of them continued trying to make their mission a success.

Their chemical attraction remained secret because somehow Mike managed to keep his expression perfectly even, his every thought hidden behind his cool, assessing eyes. And still he strove to drive her insane with hidden touches. Often. All the time, as a matter of fact. Just a finger over her skin. A whisper of a wicked smile. A brush of his thigh to the back of hers. A million different things, each designed to drive her right out of her living mind with lust.

She couldn't take it anymore. You didn't have to be a genius to know he was trying to make a point, but she was already hot and aroused every single second of every single day, so she couldn't figure out what that point was supposed to be.

After one particularly long, hot, frustrating day, after spending hours and hours attempting to coax one of the robotic arms to do as it was told, Corrine snapped. She and Mike had been side by side for hours at a time. All that time she'd been breathing his scent, feeling his own frustration mount.

He was currently on his stomach, stretched out on the platform, toying with the apparatus they were trying to operate, *trying* being the operative word. Jimmy and Frank were below him; Stephen was in the control room watching the computer images. All of them were deep in concentration. Only Mike drew her gaze.

His dark hair was ruffled, from fingers plowing through it, no doubt. His sleeves had been shoved up long ago, revealing tough, sinewy forearms, tense with strain. Every muscle in his sleek back was delineated and outlined by his damp shirt. That back alone stole her breath, then she allowed her eyes to drop lower.

It shocked her how easily he pulled her out of

work mode. This had to stop or she was simply going to go up in smoke.

At the end of the day, she calmly—or so she told herself—followed him out into the hall. "I can't do this," she said to his retreating back, making him stop. "I'm so on edge I can't stand myself, Mike. We have to…"

She steeled herself to look cool and composed, but he whipped around and grabbed her hand, opened another door, to a storage closet, then pulled her into the dark space.

"Mike—"

His name was pretty much all she got out before he hauled her up against him and kissed her, hard. It took her exactly one instant to wrap herself around him like a second skin and kiss him back, just as hard.

Something happened in that desperate moment. It became so much more than a kiss, and far more necessary than breathing. Closing her eyes to the dark around them, to the fact that this was really, really stupid, Corrine concentrated only on Mike, on his rough groan as he felt her with his hands, at the taste of him, at the contact of his big, hard body against hers. After a long heated moment, during which their hands fought with clothing to get as close as possible, she came up for air. "Mike."

He pressed his forehead to hers, his breathing ragged. "I know." He thrust his hips to hers, his frustration evident in the size of his erection.

"Mike…"

"Please, Corrine, don't turn back into the commander. Not yet. You just sounded so…turned on. I had to touch you."

Touch her he had. Her body was still thrumming with a burning desire, on the very edge, but she pulled back. He sighed and dropped his hands.

"You go first," he said, sounding strapped for air. "I'll stagger out when I can walk. It should only take about an hour."

She smoothed her clothing, imagining how she must look, all rosy and swollen-lipped. "We have to stop. You have to stop."

"Stop what, exactly?"

"Stop…touching me. You know, brushing up against me by accident."

"We happen to work within very close confines."

"Yeah, well, it doesn't have to be *that* close. And stop looking at me," she added, ignoring his startled laugh. "I mean it. You look at me and I can't think, Mike."

"Stop touching you, stop looking at you. Is it okay if I still breathe?"

Now she'd hurt his feelings again. "I'm sorry."

"Just go, Corrine."

With as much dignity as she could, she went, horrified by her yearning to dive back into the closet and attack him like a hormonal teenager. And horrified that anyone, anyone at all, could have innocently opened the storage closet and found them, locked in their ridiculous, uncontrollable passion.

8

PASSION WAS ONE GREAT BIG mystery to Corrine.

She'd felt it to some degree over the years of her adult life, but only in a limited way. Such an irrational emotion required letting go of the reins of control. While she could loosen her grip on those reins, she'd never entirely let go.

As a result, when it came to matters of the heart, she'd always been able to take it or leave it.

This time, however, there was no taking it or leaving it. *It* had taken *her*, and it had the clamp of a bulldog's jaws.

But she hadn't been born stubborn for nothing. She was tenacious, too, and if she wanted to walk away from what she felt for Mike, well then, she'd walk away. She was in control.

This was her life.

She had to repeat that to herself during the next week, often. They were deeply embroiled in the mission, working with prototypes of their real cargo. At the moment, they were trying to nail down the unloading process—a tricky, dangerous, huge undertaking complicated by the fact that no one had ever done it before.

Daily run-throughs were critical. If they messed up in space, not only would they toss away billions of dollars, they would further delay the completion of the International Space Station, perhaps indefinitely.

Couldn't happen. As a result, total and complete dedication was essential. Corrine was certain she had her team's total concentration; her own was debatable. Horrifying, the way her mind wandered. Horrifying and humiliating, because more often than not, where it wandered was straight into the gutter.

She wanted Mike, and she wanted him naked.

"Commander's mumbling to herself again," Frank said from far above, on the platform that put him at eye level with the robotic arm they were still attempting to master.

Jimmy, on his belly next to Mike, who was also spread out on the platform, brow furrowed as he worked, laughed. "She always mutters."

"I do not." Corrine climbed the ladder to reach them. Everything in this hanger was to scale, which meant huge. If she let herself think like a civilian, look around with an untrained eye, she felt like an ant.

"Actually, you do," Stephen called up from ground level, where he was watching the computer monitor carefully. "You mutter a lot. It's how we gauge your mood."

Mike, all stretched out, muscles bunching and unbunching as he worked, laughed, but bit back his smile when she looked at him with a raised brow. "I don't know anything," he said, going back to his work.

Yeah, right.

At least they didn't know *what* she'd been muttering about. There was some relief in that she'd managed to keep everything a secret.

They'd managed.

She had to give Mike credit for that, because for whatever reason, he'd abided by her wishes. She watched him now, watched as for the first time they managed to slide the robotic arm— with Mike on it—into the absolutely precise spot, the one that would allow the solar panels to be correctly unloaded.

Perfect.

It was a huge accomplishment, worthy of a celebration, and as a huge smile split her face, Corrine turned to her team. They turned to each other.

Jimmy slapped Frank on the back. Stephen whooped and hollered, then high-fived the other men when they came down.

Corrine watched, a pang in her heart, until Mike came down, too, and craned his neck.

Across the twenty feet or so that separated them, he looked right at her. The ever-present heat was still there, simmering and igniting a slow burn in the pit of her belly, but there was more, too. There was the thrill of what they'd done, and the need to share it with each other.

He took a step toward her, a slow smile curving his lips.

Everything within her tightened in anticipation.

Then Stephen reached out for Mike, halting his progress, and the connection was broken.

Corrine stepped closer, wanting to join the testosterone-fest, be part of the backslapping and whooping.

But while they all turned to her, still smiling, still proud and filled with excitement, each one of them refrained from physical contact. It didn't help to know it was her own damn fault, that she'd kept them on the wrong side of her personal brick wall.

It also didn't help to watch Mike, so excited, and so damn sexy with it. How was it that he could be so comfortable in his own skin, all the time? He fit into this world like a piece of the puzzle, and why shouldn't he?

He had a penis.

Great. She was in her thirties and had penis envy. Pathetic.

She turned away, and had nearly made it to the door before she felt the touch on her elbow. She didn't need to look to know it was Mike, that he'd somehow broken free of the pack. Not when her entire body shivered at that light touch.

What would he say, she wondered wildly, if she told him what she'd just discovered about herself, that she was jealous, pathetically jealous of what he so effortlessly had with the team? That she no longer enjoyed her solitude?

"Corrine," he said in a low, husky voice that scraped at every raw nerve and made her shudder again. "We did it."

"I know." She didn't look at him, couldn't.

He touched her again. Standing behind her as

he was, with his back to the team, no one could see how he stroked the small of her back. Just a few fingers, nothing more, and it shook her to the core.

"I'm going to go upstairs." To the control room. Where there would be more ecstatic people, but them she could handle. "I want to see if—"

"*We did it,* Corrine. I think that deserves a hug, don't you? Or maybe even more. What do you think?"

Nervous now, she let out a little laugh. "You're crazy. I can't touch you here."

"Why not? The rest of us did."

Had he read her mind, or was she just that transparent when it came to him?

"Why would anyone think anything of it?" he asked reasonably.

Yes, why would they? All sorts of excuses danced in her head, but at the root of all of them came the truth. "It's not them, it's me. I don't know what happens to me around you."

"I do. I threaten your sense of control." His broad chest brushed her shoulder. "You threaten mine right back. Did you ever think of that?"

She studied the door. "No."

"This isn't going to go away," he said quietly. "We might as well just go with it."

"You mean sleep together again."

"Hell, yes," he said fervently.

She laughed then, but since it sounded half-hysterical, she brought her hands up to her mouth. "Oh, God, Mike. I don't know what to do with you."

He turned her to face him, looking deep into her eyes. "Yes you do. You know exactly what to do." When she only stared at him, probably wild-eyed and wide-eyed, he let out a long, slow breath. "You're torturing me. You know that?"

"*I'm* torturing *you*?"

"All these stolen touches and wild kisses—"

"Then stop—"

"I look at you with your hair up, in these severe clothes, and I want to see the *other* Corrine. Without the mask of the job, without the icy control. It makes me ache."

"Mike—"

"*Ache*," he whispered. "I'm staying at the Hyatt hotel. Suite—"

"No," she quickly gasped, putting a finger to his mouth. "Don't tell me—"

"Six forty-four," he said around her fingers. He

grinned. "Sixth floor again. Can you believe the irony? I'm hoping it's a lucky sign."

She groaned and closed her eyes. "I didn't want to know that."

"Yes, you did."

Yeah, damn it, she did.

AS IF FATE WAS MOCKING her, the day ended early, leaving Corrine with two choices. She could go home and see what she could cook up for dinner.

Or she could catch a movie, as she'd been wanting to do for months.

She pulled up to her complex and stared at the building. She hadn't gone food shopping; she'd have to make due with cold cereal and the television for company.

Mmm, so appealing.

Well, it was her own fault, being so wrapped up in work that she no longer had a private life. She could go see her parents, who'd welcome her with open arms. But much as she loved them, that didn't appeal at the moment, either.

Going to the Hyatt to see what Mike wanted, now that appealed.

Only she knew what he wanted; yes, she knew exactly. It was the same thing she wanted.

But what then? Would this almost desperate need for him go away?

Telling herself it would, it had to, because she couldn't stand it otherwise, she ran into her condo to change, then ran right back out again and drove toward the hotel.

THE KNOCK AT THE DOOR startled Mike. His heart began to race, and though he told himself it could be anyone, anyone at all, he hurried toward the door, holding his breath, wondering, hoping...

And then he was looking into Corrine's eyes and seeing everything he felt mirrored right back at him: need and wariness, and even fear.

"I don't know what's happening to my perfectly planned out life," she said, clearly baffled. "I can't concentrate, can't think, can't do anything except daydream about you, and—" she straightened and pointed at him "—it's all your fault."

"That's funny."

"There's nothing funny about this."

"It's funny because I'm having the same problem," he said. "And I was pretty certain it was all *your* fault."

She let out a little disbelieving laugh. "Yeah, right. You're having the same problem."

"Can't eat, can't sleep, yadda, yadda," he said, narrowing his eyes when she laughed again. "Now *you're* amused."

"Yes, because you're having no trouble at all concentrating and thinking! I know because I've been watching you. You look cool, calm and collected, and I've got to tell you, Mike, it's really ticking me off."

Now *he* laughed. And hauled her close, taking her mouth, her body and his own life into his hands, because he was going to have her again, he had to have her, and now. Given the hungry sound that ripped from her throat, she felt the same way.

He deepened the kiss and she met him more than halfway. It was a bigger thrill than what they'd accomplished today at work. Sinking his fingers into her hair, he freed it from the clip that held it captive. She dug her fingers into his scalp, too, holding his head prisoner to the kiss he didn't want to escape from, anyway. They were gravitating toward something hot and out of control, their bodies sliding and grinding against each another, their hands fighting for purchase, when Corrine pulled back to draw a breath. He pulled back, too, and she bit his lower lip. Heat spiraled through him and he reached for the zipper on her sweater.

But she put her hands over his.

Barely able to see through the sexual haze she'd created, he shook his head. "We're stopping?"

Her breathing was as uneven as his strained voice, her eyes glazed, her mouth full and wet. She looked very uncommanderlike, and he thoroughly enjoyed that. "We're right in the open doorway, Mike."

Oh. Oh yeah. He'd forgotten. They could have been on the moon for all he remembered. "See? Proof positive you make me lose my mind." He pulled her in, stopping only to slam the door before leading her to the king-size bed.

She came to a grinding halt, staring at it. "Are we making another mistake?"

Hell yes, but he wasn't about to admit that now, so he pulled her around and kissed her again, kissed her long and thoroughly, until he could barely recall his name and knew she couldn't either. Then and only then did he go for the prize once again—the zipper on the form-fitting sweater she wore. His knuckles brushed her skin as he worked it down, down, down, discovering halfway that his sexy commander wore nothing beneath. Bending, he put his mouth to her throat. Her eyes slid shut as he nipped and sucked his way down to the base of her neck.

"Mike...wait."

He tasted her soft, creamy flesh.

She moaned.

"Now?" he asked hopefully, still tugging on the zipper.

"I don't know." She pulled his T-shirt free of his waistband and over his head. Then stood blinking at his chest. "How come you're so perfectly made?" she asked seriously, lifting her hand to run her fingers over the muscles that twitched with her every touch.

"God designed man this way so despite our stupidity, women couldn't resist us. Is it working?"

She nodded slowly. "Undoubtedly."

"I'm sorry I'm hurting you at work, Corrine. I don't mean to be."

"I know." She stared at his body with what looked like befuddled arousal.

"Now?" he asked in a voice very close to begging as he fingered the zipper between her breasts.

"Okay," she whispered. "Now."

Ziiip. He spread the sweater open, pushing the material from her shoulders to hang from her elbows. Looking down at her, he found even his ragged breathing went still. Everything went still, except his heart, which chose this moment to ache like hell. "You take my breath away, Corrine."

She put a hand over the one he'd pressed to his heart. "Mike—"

"No, I mean it. Look at you." Reverently, he reached out and touched the tip of one beaded nipple. She let out a sexy, helpless little sound that nearly did him in. "I want to drop to my knees and worship you for..." *The rest of my life.*

"Kiss me, Mike."

"But..." He wanted to think about this, discuss it.

"Kiss." As if she'd read his thoughts and had been equally terrified, she hauled him close. "Just shut up and kiss me." Making sure he complied, she glued her mouth to his, making love to it with her tongue, sliding in and out in a motion he didn't even try to resist, and within moments

they were clinging to each other. He couldn't touch enough of her, and when he tried harder, she lifted a leg to his hip, pressing the heat of her to him, gliding over him until his eyes crossed.

"Okay, we've got to get horizontal," he decided breathlessly. "Before we kill each other." Tipping her to the bed, he crawled up her body, spreading her legs to make a place for himself between them.

Corrine pushed her hips up, meeting his erection more than halfway. Somehow her skirt had gotten shoved up to her waist, leaving only the silky barrier of her panties between them, but the friction of that, along with the helpless but insistent thrust of her hips, nearly did him in.

Nearly. Because while she took his breath, she'd also somehow taken his heart. He wanted to talk, wanted to know what was happening, wanted to know why he suddenly felt as though maybe it was far more than simple, unquenchable heat they were generating right here on this bed. Only she grabbed his ears and pulled his mouth back to hers, keeping it busy while she pumped and rocked her hips against the biggest hard-on he'd ever sported.

"Now," she demanded, panting. If she could

have heard herself, she'd have been horrified, but she couldn't hear, couldn't do anything but feel. Sensation after sensation rocked through her, and she found herself holding on by a thread as his greedy, talented mouth ravaged hers. When they broke apart for air, he slid down her body, opening his lips wide around her nipple, using his tongue and his teeth to exact more dark, needy sounds from her. She watched helplessly as he drove her further toward the edge with just that tongue. Then his big, rough hand worked its way down her belly, beneath the edging of her panties. Lifting his head, he gauged her reaction closely as his finger unerringly located the exact spot designed to drive her to the brink.

She made some unintelligible sound, which turned into a moan when he lightly feathered it with the pad of his thumb. Her every nerve ending throbbed and pulsed and begged for more, but the fact was, she was out of her league. She had no clue, no road map and no guidance. She was parachuting without a damn parachute. "Wait!"

"I don't think so, not now." He touched and stroked and mastered her, whipping her into a desperate frenzy. Staring down at her, his eyes were dark with desire. "You wanted this." With the finger that had become the center of her universe, he circled her opening, once, twice, making her cry out and move convulsively against his hand. "Didn't you?"

"Yes," she gasped, thrashing on the bed. "Yes, I wanted this!"

Galvanized into action, he stripped off his jeans, then made her clothes vanish as well. He ripped open a condom, his gaze devouring her as he put it on. Shamelessly needy, she pulled her knees back, opening herself to him in a way that was utterly foreign to her, but felt so right at the moment.

His eyes all but gobbled her up. "You are so beautiful. And so mine." He pushed into her, just a little, just an inch, dragging a whimper of need out of her.

"More." She thrust up to meet him.

"Oh, yeah. More." He pulled his hips back slightly, and another little whimper shuddered in her throat, but then he thrust again, deeper this time. And then deeper still. And again, until he was so far seated inside her that she couldn't tell where she ended and he began.

He held himself still, then, looking down at her as a parade of emotions crossed his face: dazed wonder, harsh need.

"Mike," she whispered, feeling all those emotions right back, and he thrust into her harder, deeper, over and over again. Her head fell back. She arched up into him. She was dying. *"Mike."*

"Right here, baby. Come." He delved a thumb into the wet tangle of curls above where they were joined, stroking as she writhed beneath him. "Come for me."

He was watching her. Waiting. Egging on all that sensation inside her until it came to a roaring explosion. She'd never been watched before. It should have stopped her cold, should have left her unable to fall apart, screaming, panting, making an unholy fool of herself as she shuddered and jerked under the assault of ecstasy, but it didn't.

And when she could breathe again, she realized she hadn't been the only one to completely lose herself. He'd collapsed against her, having banded his arms tight around her, holding her to him in a bone-crushing grip.

Amazingly enough, they fell asleep like that.

MIKE WOKE with a wide, canary-eating grin and yet another erection. Turning toward Corrine, already thinking about exactly what he intended to do to her, he stopped, shocked into immobility.

She was gone.

Again.

Damn her! And damn him for allowing it. He should have handcuffed her to the headboard. Should have never fallen asleep.

Should have...should have...should have. The truth was, there was nothing he could do to keep her, nothing at all.

Unless she wanted to be kept.

Which she didn't.

9

MIKE WALKED INTO the conference room and Corrine's heart took off like a rocket. "Good morning," she said coolly. No one had to know she was on the verge of death by mortification, or that her palms were damp with nerves, just from seeing him again.

She'd left him blissfully, gloriously naked, fully sated and fast asleep. He'd accuse her of being a chicken, but it hadn't been fear that made her run; it had simply been time to put aside all personal stuff and get to work.

Here at work, she couldn't afford to be thinking of someone else, grieving over what could never be. Concentration was required. Time to put everything else aside and get on with her scheduled team meeting.

No problem. Putting everything else aside had always come easy for Corrine.

Until now.

Mike didn't answer or return her greeting, didn't even acknowledge it. He looked tall, dark and royally pissed off, not to mention so beautiful he took her breath away.

"Um...coffee?" she asked, gesturing toward the pot. The few sips she'd already taken were making her jittery.

Or maybe that was Mike.

"No, thanks."

She busied herself adding sugar and cream to her coffee, though she preferred it black. But she needed in the worst way to not look at him.

"Corrine."

He was going to want to talk about it. She should have known.

"Corrine." His eyes glittered with attitude and knowledge, knowledge that she'd run from him. Which really was proof positive that he could never understand her. His dark hair was still wet from what must have been a very recent shower, one in which he hadn't shaved, as witnessed by the dark, day-old stubble on his jaw.

She knew that stubble, knew it intimately, knew how it felt gliding over her skin, the raspy sound it made when he lingered, and the citrusy scent of it.

"Don't," he said in a gruff, almost harsh voice, and she was thankful they were the only ones in the room, because that voice made her blood start singing.

"Don't what?" she asked as lightly as she could.

"Don't look at me as if you can't take your eyes off me, because we both know that's not true."

It *was* true, but she wasn't about to admit that. "I'm only looking at you because you're early. I'm surprised, is all."

"I'm early," he said, stalking toward her with his long-gaited, very confident stride. "Because I woke up early. With a raging hard-on, as a matter of fact."

She bit her lip and held her ground, forcing her chin up so she would look fearless. Which she absolutely was. Fearless. Nothing got to her, nothing…except for maybe, just maybe, this man. "I thought all men woke up that way."

"Yes, but I woke up expecting to be wrapped around a warm, sleepy woman." He was nearly upon her now. "One whom I could slowly caress and kiss and taste until she was wide awake and writhing beneath me, making those soft, desperate sounds, which, by the way, are the sexiest I've ever heard."

"Mike—"

"And then when I had her that way," he continued in a soft, silky voice, "I was going to slowly sink inside her, one inch at a time, until—"

"Stop," she whispered desperately, weakly, glancing at the open doorway. But no one else had arrived yet. She was shaking, damp from perspiration, just at his words!

Did she really sound soft and desperate when he was buried deep inside her?

And did he really think she was sexy? No one had ever told her such things. No one had ever even thought them of her, she was quite certain. "We can't do this here."

"Oh, yes, we can." His eyes were flashing, and despite his unbearably sensuous words and soft tone, his mouth was grim. "We can do this here, because you're not going to let me do it anywhere else. I might be a little slow on the uptake, Corrine, but I'm not stupid."

No, no he wasn't. And he really was furious. She supposed he had a right, but she had a right, too. And damn it, hadn't she told him nothing could come of this…this *thing* between them? It wasn't as if she'd led him on, or purposely set out to hurt anyone's feelings. Besides, if anyone was going to get hurt here, it was going to be her. Because she couldn't fool herself any longer; he was magnificent. And he wouldn't stay single for long. Some other woman would come along and snag him.

But she…she would forever pine over what might have been. "I realize you're upset—"

"Upset," he repeated in a quiet, reasonable voice. He even nodded. But he didn't stop coming toward her. "Yes, you're right about that, Corrine. I'm upset."

"I know." Not allowing herself to back up, she reached behind her and gripped the conference table for support. "I do know. But—"

"No, I don't think you do." He stopped a breath away from her, so close she had to tip her head back to see into his face, but no way was she going to retreat.

She retreated for no one.

"I'm beginning to realize you know nothing about me or my feelings," he said. "Nothing at all. In fact…" He tipped his head and studied her for a long, squirmy moment. "Maybe you really are the Ice Queen everyone says you are."

She couldn't even open her mouth, his words cut such a deep wound. Her hand came up to rub at the sudden ache in her chest and she was half surprised to find no sign of blood. "You...you think I'm an Ice Queen."

"Look me in the eyes and tell me you're not. Tell me you're not frozen to the emotions running wild within me. Do it," he begged softly, reaching out, trying to make her look at him. But she was done. Done with this, and done with him, because damn it, he didn't understand at all, and she wasn't about to try to make him.

Not when all her life she'd had to explain herself, except with her family. They'd always accepted her just as she was, and she'd always believed that someday, somewhere, she'd find that same acceptance elsewhere. And when she did, she'd always promised herself, that would be the man she'd marry.

It had never happened, not yet anyway, and she was beginning to believe it never would. Another bitter disappointment, knowing love, true love, always eluded her.

"Corrine."

His voice was so soft, so urgent, so utterly gripping. She lifted her head, but Stephen entered the room just then, followed by Frank.

"Ready to rock and roll?" Frank asked, rubbing his hands together with glee. Nothing made Frank happier than a SIM, which was what they were going to be doing directly after their team meeting.

"Let's get to it," Stephen said, the two of them oblivious to the tension in the room.

Jimmy came in next, his eyes suddenly measured and assessing as he looked back and forth between the commander and pilot. "What's going on?"

"Nothing," Corrine said quickly. Too quickly, damn it. She felt herself starting to crumble. They could see something, some crack in her control, and she knew it would be beyond awful if she didn't get it together right here, right now. "We're just getting ready for the meeting, going over some notes."

Jimmy's eyebrows came together as he studied her. And now Frank and Stephen were more closely assessing her as well.

"Did we miss something?"

"Yeah. The doughnuts," Mike said, shocking

Corrine with his rescue, especially since she'd jumped all over him the last time he'd done that.

"There were doughnuts and you ate them all?" Stephen sighed. "You owe me, Wright."

"Two kinds of people on this team," Mike said, still looking at Corrine. "The quick and the hungry."

Frank laughed. "Well, color me hungry then."

"Damn," Jimmy said, pulling out a chair.

Stephen waggled a finger beneath Mike's nose. "You're buying lunch, pal. With dessert."

Corrine managed a smile as she grabbed her clipboard. "Lunch is on me. We'll be needing to calorie up for this afternoon's SIM."

Among the pretend groans and eye rolling, she dared a glance at Mike. He looked back at her steadily, and utterly without expression.

Not once since they'd first met had the heat and even basic affection been gone from his gaze. Not once.

It was gone now. Good. Just as she'd wanted.

But her throat burned and her chest felt tight as a drum. And for the first time, she had to wonder what she'd sacrificed in the name of success and her job.

FOR THE NEXT MONTH Corrine didn't have time to so much as breathe, nor did anyone else associated with the mission.

Still, Mike was everywhere—in her SIM, in her meetings, at her side...and in her dreams.

At work they did nothing but simulation after simulation. Everything from this point on would be a run-through of the upcoming mission, only a month away now. Everything they did, they did as a team.

So she was constantly with Mike.

Her frozen heart, along with all its complicated, newly defrosted emotions, left her with no defenses. During one particularly grueling afternoon, when things weren't going right, her first instinct was to bark out orders and get the team back on track. But two words stopped her.

Ice Queen.

Walking the length of the hangar, consulting her clipboard and trying to smooth out a dozen things at once, she happened to catch sight of herself, reflected in a shiny control panel.

Her hair was clipped back, not a strand out of place. She wore little makeup and no smile, making her appear...stern.

The Ice Queen.

Around her was controlled chaos as her team prepared for yet another simulated flight, but she went stock-still. Was she really as stern as she looked? She didn't want to think so. She was as fun-loving and full of joy as anyone else.

So why did she look so hard? Pulling her lips back, she attempted a smile, but it didn't reach her eyes. Standing there, she tried to think of something funny, something that would evoke a genuine smile. Leaning closer to her reflection, she racked her brain and—

"Need a mirror, Commander?"

The half-ass smile froze in place. Moving her eyes from her reflection to the one that had appeared right next to her, she groaned.

Mike, of course.

"What are you doing?" She straightened up as if she hadn't just been practicing ridiculous smiles at herself in the reflective panel of a space shuttle.

"Watching you watch yourself." He leaned back, making himself comfortable. He was always comfortable, damn him. "That's some smile you've got there, Commander."

"Why do you keep calling me that?"

"Because that's what you are, remember? My commander. Nothing more, nothing less."

Well. Her own doing, that, so there was no reason to get her feelings hurt.

"You ought to try using it more." For just a moment, his eyes roamed over her face like a sweet touch, before he caught himself and looked away. "The smile, that is."

She'd used her smile plenty with him, mostly in bed. At that thought, she bent down, pretending to study a panel, but it was merely an excuse to gather herself. Yet the facade she wore like a coat wouldn't work this time, because it would only prove his point.

Oh hell, why did she even care? She didn't. She'd just have to be the woman she always was, and if he chose to misunderstand, then so much the better. It would remind her of her own foolishness.

While she was hunkered down, contemplating all this, a hand appeared in front of her face. Mike's hand. She stared at those reaching fingers. With any other man, she'd have taken the gesture as an insult, because she could get up herself and always had. But with Mike, she knew it had nothing at all to do with her capabilities, or his perception of them. He was simply being a gentleman.

Which meant she was a lady, at least in his eyes. Well, she'd been a lady and more with him, hadn't she?

Silently she took his hand and rose. Together they joined the team on the other side of the hangar, and all moved into place for their SIM.

For this particular exercise—simulating the landing at the space station, the "parking" and the subsequent unloading—Mike and she had to sit side by side in a relatively small space, with little natural light, mostly just the blue-green glare from the glowing controls. Even the air felt constricted, creating an intimate ambience that was almost too much to take.

With every passing second, as Corrine worked the controls, she became more and more aware of him. She couldn't even breathe without his scent filling her lungs. Did he mean to be so overwhelming with his presence? Did he know that his dark eyes drew her, that every time he swallowed, his Adam's apple danced and she felt the insane urge to put her mouth to that very spot? Did he know that his rolled-up sleeves, so carelessly shoved up his strong arms, made her want to reach out and touch? That when she leaned to the right, her shoulder brushed his broader, stronger one? And that she kept doing it on purpose for the small thrill of it?

He didn't look at her, but had dropped into the "zone" where he was utterly calm and totally focused, ready for anything.

As she should have been.

She'd nearly managed it when their fingers tangled as they both reached for the same control.

Her eye caught his, and though he was completely into his work, something flickered there, warmed.

It should be against the code of space travel to be so sexy, she thought, and turned away to focus on unloading the cargo.

And when, two minutes later, one of the solar panels malfunctioned during the unfurling, it took her a moment to understand it wasn't her fault, that it had nothing to do with what she was feeling for her pilot.

The broken equipment was only a prototype for the *real* component, one of three that had been built for exactly these practice missions, but that made it no less of a problem. It required sending hordes of engineers back to the drawing board, soothing freaked-out NASA officials and dealing with the press, who were dying to put a negative spin on the price of the space program.

Hours and hours later, when Corrine finally took a moment to draw a deep breath, she escaped to the staff kitchen.

Mike had gotten there first.

He said nothing, just lifted the milk carton he held as if in a silent toast.

A job well done? Is that what he meant? "Thanks for your hard work today," she said.

He took a long swig, then licked his upper lip. "You worked harder than any of us. Did anyone thank *you*?"

"No."

"They should have." He stayed where he was, which was unlike him, but then again, she'd made it pretty clear that's what she wanted. A lot of space between them. "Then thank you," he said simply. "You've done a great job."

"For an Ice Queen."

"What?"

"I've done a good job, for an Ice Queen. Isn't that what you meant?"

He actually looked surprised, then slowly shook his head. "You still stewing over that?"

Apparently so. How terribly revealing.

"I would have apologized. *Should* have apologized." He looked at her for a long second, then let out a hard breath. "I was mad at you, Corrine. I wanted to break through and see, if only for a moment, the woman beneath the tough veneer, the woman I've laughed with, talked to, made love with. I was frustrated and hot and full of temper, a bad combo on any day."

"You're saying that was just temper talking?"

"As in do I really think of you as an Ice Queen?" He stepped closer, touched her hair. "I don't want to. God, I don't want to."

But he *did*, she thought.

His voice lowered. Softened. Became irresistible. "I hurt you. I'm sorry for that, Corrine. So sorry."

He was sorry, which left her floundering, because without her anger, everything else pushed and shoved its way to the surface. It was that everything else she couldn't handle.

As USUAL, she slept alone, haunted by dreams of warm, loving arms holding her, pressing her against a long, hard, muscled body that knew exactly how to give and what to take.

She woke up hot, damp and frustrated, and wrapped around her pillow.

A bad start, to say the least, and the day didn't improve from there. A critical communications program, brand-new for this mission, crashed. Another catastrophe, and another rush for the drawing board.

By the end of the day she was tense, tired and maybe more than a tad irritable. Grumbling to herself, she went to the staff room for scalding, black coffee…and ran into Mike.

He wasn't drinking milk this time, wasn't doing anything but standing near the coffeepot. She wondered if maybe he'd been waiting there for her.

"You going to thank me again for a job well done?" she asked, more than a little caustically. She couldn't help it. If ever she'd deserved her Ice Queen title, it had been today. "After all, I've worked pretty damn hard these past hours, yelling at computer programmers, scaring engineers, terrorizing rogue reporters, etcetera."

"Yeah, I'm going to thank you." He smiled at her dare, deflating her anger with nothing more than his presence. "You saved our butts today.

You saved our butts yesterday, too, and you know what? I think you're magnificent."

"I..." How did he do that, render her speechless? "I don't know what to say to you."

His mouth curved. "You never do, when it comes to a compliment."

The way he looked at her made her suddenly long for the simplicity of what they shared only when they were in bed.

His eyes darkened. "I'd give anything to hear your thought, the one that made your cheeks flush hot."

"Not a chance."

"Damn."

"I figured you were still mad at me."

"Mad?" He slowly shook his head. "I've been a lot of things when it comes to you, most of which you don't want to hear, so think good and hard, Corrine, before you open up this can of worms."

She might have done just that, if her beeper hadn't suddenly gone off. An emergency page, she discovered, which didn't bode well.

What else can go wrong? she wondered, rushing through the maze of hallways.

"Anything," Mike said grimly, startling her,

because she hadn't realized he'd come along or that she'd spoken out loud.

It was the robotic arm, they discovered a few moments later, which was now malfunctioning after Stephen's weight had been on it, while he was working on a relaying function.

"Defunct," Stephen called down in disgust.

The arm, too, was just a prototype, but a malfunction was a malfunction. Corrine didn't hesitate to climb up, pushing aside all the technicians to get there. Then dug right in, barking suggestions and orders, and more suggestions.

Two hours later, they'd solved the problem. By the time Corrine climbed down, she was exhausted, had a headache and could eat a horse.

Mike wasn't in the kitchen this time as she finally grabbed her things and prepared to go home, but he was in the parking lot, getting into his rental car.

When he saw her, he went still, carefully studying her face for a long moment.

Always uncomfortable with scrutiny, she shifted. "What? Why are you looking at me like that?"

"Nothing. Forget it." But he pocketed his keys and moved toward her with that long-legged stride of his. He'd worked all day, too, right by her side, but he didn't look as rumpled as she felt, not at all. His sleeves were still shoved back, and maybe his shirt was a little wrinkled from where he'd been crawling around on the robotic arm alongside her, but he looked…well, unbearably familiar, and unbearably sexy.

Reaching out, he tucked a stray strand of hair behind her ear. "You look beat."

His voice was low, soft. Gentle. His fingers on her cheek, where they lingered, were tender.

Damn him for all the inconsistencies! And damn him for still, after all this time, being able to melt her with nothing more than a half smile and the touch of a finger on her skin.

"You're an amazing woman, Corrine," he said quietly, with a different light in his gaze than she'd ever seen before. Was that…respect she saw there now? Respect and—oh God, he was leaning down to kiss her. Just once, and ever so softly.

It took everything she had not to cling to that soft, yet firm mouth.

Yes, it *was* respect in his gaze; she could see that now as he pulled back. And even more irresistible, there was heart, too.

Terrifying, that heart and its emotions, because she'd never received that from anyone other than her family before. She couldn't resist. "Mike."

Slipping his fingers along her jaw, he skimmed the pad of his thumb over her lips, holding her words in. "Night, Corrine."

As she watched him drive away, standing there alone in the NASA parking lot, she had to face an uncomfortable realization.

Her life wasn't nearly as complete as she thought it was, not now that she understood some of what she was missing.

10

THEY WERE IN THE FINAL stages, coming into the home stretch before the launch. With a month left to go, Mike's days were wild, chaotic and nerve-racking. They were the most exciting days of his life.

Exhausting, too. He couldn't remember the last time he'd had a full night's sleep and a decent meal, but he wouldn't have changed his life at the moment for anything.

Well, actually, he amended, looking across the large hangar to where he could see Corrine pointing and directing several crew members, there was one thing he would change if he could.

His relationship with Corrine.

It had started out on a whim, that night three months ago. A thrilling sexual adventure, and it had flamed hot and bright. *Still* flamed hot and bright, only now she pretended it didn't exist, and he'd let her.

He'd been willing to let her pretend forever, thinking no woman, no matter how great in bed, was worth the upheaval that the demanding, incorrigible, unforgiving, passionate, determined Corrine Atkinson would cause in his life.

But that had been when he'd considered only the sexual nature of their relationship. Now, after working with her day in and day out, for weeks and weeks, he felt differently. He knew what it took to make her smile, even laugh. Knew how to make her entire face light up with the thrill of what they were doing. Knew how she thought, and what she wanted out of her day.

And incredibly, he could no longer remember what it was to want her only physically, because that want had deepened. Grown. Hell, it had *skyrocketed*, if the truth was told.

He wanted it all.

Their day was done now, and it was actually early enough that if he wanted, he could go home and have a life until bedtime. But he didn't want to go home—not alone, anyway.

He wanted the company of a woman. Not just any woman, but one he knew, and who knew him. One who could simply look at him and know that he needed her body close to his, her arms around his neck and her mouth curved in a smile just for him.

Corrine. He wanted Corrine.

Slowly, he walked toward her, watching as everyone called out their good-nights to her. For most she had parting words, advice, comments, commands, and it made him smile.

He couldn't believe it, but along the way, he'd actually come to enjoy the fact that she was higher ranked than him. He liked her demanding ways. In fact, at this moment, he ached for her to look at him, with her will of steel, and demand something special of him. Of course, he doubted she'd think his thoughts appropriate—or his erection, for that matter. *Tough luck.*

She and Stephen were high above him now, on a platform. They were studying the west bay of the shuttle prototype. Corrine was pointing, using her hands as she talked. As always, she was oblivious to the height, to the danger, to how absolutely appealing she looked. Any other woman would be…but she *wasn't* any other woman.

After another few minutes, Stephen came down, looking beat. When he saw Mike, he shook his head. "I need sleep, even if she doesn't," he grumbled, and left.

When Corrine came down, he could see she was lost in thought, probably calculating something in her head, or formulating some new way to torture her team tomorrow. Whatever it was, it gave him the advantage, as she clearly believed herself alone.

She hopped off the last rung of the ladder, turned and plowed right into him. Stiffening, she gasped.

Mike used the opportunity to put his hands on her arms in the pretext of holding her steady, though there was no one steadier than Corrine Atkinson.

"Mike."

"In the flesh." His fingers brushed the bare skin of her forearms, then slid up beneath her short sleeves to skim over her shoulders.

She shivered. "What are you doing?"

"Working for a woman is very satisfying, did you know that?"

"Mike."

"Know what else? I've been unfair to both of us, letting us get away with ignoring each other."

"Don't be silly, we—" She broke off with a harsh intake of breath when his thumbs brushed the sides of her breasts. "Stop that."

"Think how good an orgasm would be for your stress level right now."

"Mike!"

Because she smelled so good, and looked so annoyed, yet bewildered, he rubbed his jaw against hers. He'd meant only to soothe, but like a cat, she stretched against him, and the thought of soothing fled from his mind, replaced by something far deeper. And hotter.

Concentrate, he told himself. *Screw this up now and you won't get another chance.* "I don't want you to ignore me anymore."

"We haven't been ignoring each other. As you've mentioned, we work together, every single day."

"You know what I mean. You think you can't let anyone in your life, that you have to be one big, bad, tough woman to make it in this world." Beneath his hands, she stiffened, and he touched her face lightly, lifting her chin up to look into her eyes. "Any response to that?"

"I'm considering several."

Because her eyes were flashing and her body was tense, he held her tight, knowing, now, that she held black belts in several different martial arts. "Okay, let's skip to me," he said quickly. "I believed I didn't need anyone in my life because it was so full already. Women had a place there, but it wasn't a very big one. But you know what, Corrine?"

"I can't imagine."

"I was wrong." He laughed in delight at her one raised brow. "I know, can you believe it? *Wrong.* Dead wrong. And guess what, baby? You were wrong, too."

"I don't know what you're talking about."

"Oh, yes, you do." He smiled, feeling some sympathy because he understood the fear that he knew was coursing through her veins. He understood it well. "This has been a long time coming," he murmured, wondering just how alone they were, and whether, if he kissed her now, he'd ever be able to stop. But he cupped her face, tilted it to suit him, and bent. She slapped a hand to his chest. "Someone will see!"

"Everyone has left." He touched her mouth with his.

She gasped and he simply used that to his advantage, deepening the kiss. When she met his tongue with her own, his knees nearly buckled. "Corrine," he whispered, pulling back to gaze into her eyes. "I know this looks impossible."

"It *is* impossible."

He set a finger to her lips. "So we work together. Lots of couples do, and—"

"*Couples?*" she choked out. "My God, Mike. We're not a couple!"

"I know, that word's hard to wrap your tongue around, much less your brain. But I can't imagine my life without you in it." He let out a harsh laugh and shook his head. "Can you believe it? Me saying those words? But it's the utter, terrifying truth. I have no idea what's happened to me—wait, I do know. It's you. *You've* happened to me. I want you, control freak or not—"

"Now, wait a minute—"

"In fact, I like that about you. You know what you want, you're not afraid to go get it, with the exception being, of course…me."

She just stared at him. "I think you inhaled too much oxygen on that last SIM."

"And you know what else?" he asked her cheerfully. "I even like that you're higher ranked than me."

"You're a sick man, Mike."

"Look, if you're worried about the people here, and what they think, this mission will be over soon enough, and then we'll both be reassigned for other missions."

"*What are you saying?*" she cried, wide-eyed. "My God, Mike, what are you saying?"

"That we should give in to what we feel for each other."

She shook her head, so sidetracked she'd forgotten he still held her. "But I don't *know* what I feel."

"Then let's explore that." Nibbling at one corner of her mouth, then the other, he slowly pulled back. Her eyes were half-closed, sleepy and sexy. Her mouth, wet from his, pulled into a pout when he didn't kiss her again, making him let out a laugh that turned into a groan when he looked down and saw her hardened nipples pressing against the fabric of her blouse. "Cold, Corrine?"

"No." Her voice was low. Almost harsh. "Damn you, I'd almost stopped dreaming about you, almost stopped waking up hot and bothered."

"Really?"

"No," she said miserably.

Now he did grin, and when she saw it, she pushed him back, walking away. "I need...air," she said over her shoulder.

Needing some himself, he followed, but she stopped in the hallway in front of her office.

She stared at the door and he stared at her slim back, wondering if she could possibly be feeling half of what he was.

Turning only her head, she looked at him, and there was no mistaking her need, her hunger. Slowly she opened the door. Flicked off the light. Stepped inside the darkened room and turned to face him. "I've obviously lost my head, but... would you care to come in?"

He moved so fast, coming in, shutting and then locking the door, fumbling with his jacket, that she let out a low laugh that was unbearably erotic in its sudden confidence. "We're really going to do this?"

"Yes." He came forward in the dim light shining through her slated blinds, to haul her close. "Now kiss me like you did in my dreams last night."

"It will help, right?" she asked. "If we appease this...this heat now? Then maybe we won't implode on our mission, when we're locked in space together for ten long days."

He didn't know how to tell her that he was beginning to suspect they'd always be this desperate for each other.

Always.

That word was a doozy. It went along with others, like *forever*.

And *love*.

Oh God. He needed to sit down.

"Mike?" Corrine nervously licked her lips in an innocent, artless way that went straight to his gut. And then his heart. And suddenly he felt strong, so very, very strong.

"Is this crazy?" she whispered, covering her face. "What are we doing?"

"What we were born to do." He took her hands and pinned them behind her, which left her body thrust against his. His voice was far thicker than it had been. "Let's make love."

"And get it out of our system."

"Hmm," he murmured noncommittally.

Corrine was beginning to wonder if that was even possible, but she couldn't think effectively with her attention so drawn to his wonderful, firm, masculine mouth. "We really shouldn't. You know that."

He drew her closer, but didn't kiss her, just

held her until her entire body was throbbing with need.

"Love that," he murmured. "The connection. Can you feel it?"

"What is *it*, exactly?" she asked, needing to know. But instead of answering, he unbuttoned her blouse, unhooked her bra, pulling the material away from her body. Then he just looked at her for a long, long moment before slowly shaking his head in wonder. Touching a nipple with his finger, he watched intently as it puckered and darkened for him. "So pretty."

Silly, really, how just a few words from him could make her lose her head. "Here, Mike?"

He smiled against her throat. "Oh yeah, here. And everywhere."

"What if someone comes?"

"Everyone is gone."

Turning, she swept everything on her desk to the floor with one swipe, watching as the piles of paper hit with a thunk. "I've always wanted to do that."

Laughing, Mike helped her up, then stepped between her thighs. He undid her slacks and slipped his hands inside her panties, holding her bottom, pulling her close to a most impressive erection.

Wrapping her arms around his neck, she pressed her face into his neck and breathed deeply of the masculine scent that had haunted her for months. With his big, warm hands he squeezed her bottom, then cupped her breasts, plumping them up, dipping his mouth down to taste, using his tongue and then his teeth until her hips jerked in reaction. "Mike."

"I know."

"Hurry."

"Take everything off, then," he said in a rough whisper, and lent his own hands to the cause. In two seconds flat they were both stripped. Corrine had barely straightened up before Mike slipped his hands between her thighs, opening them wide. "Mmm, you're wet."

Yes. Wet and hot, and she'd made his fingers that way, too, the fingers that were softly stroking, over and over again, until she was arching up into him, helplessly thrusting against that hand. "Mike!"

"Tell me."

"Don't stop." To make sure he wouldn't, that he couldn't, she closed her legs around him and that hand, shamelessly rubbing and writhing, desperate for more, for the touch that would send her reeling. "I need to—"

"Then do it," he urged, leaning down and drawing one nipple into his mouth, sucking it as he slid a finger inside her.

She would have fallen backward if he hadn't brought one hand to her waist to support her. Now that finger withdrew slowly—so slowly she thought she'd scream—only to dance over and over her with infinite, thorough patience. At every pass she cried out his name.

"Come for me," he coaxed, his mouth full of breast, his fingers diving back into her. "Come for me, baby."

And she did. She exploded. Imploded. Burst out of herself. All of that and more, and when she could hear again, see again, she realized she had him in a death grip and was still chanting his name.

Mike was breathing every bit as harshly as she. Lifting his head, he looked at her, his eyes hot and dark, so very dark.

Cupping his face, she kissed him. "We're not done."

He smiled and sighed reverently, pulling a little packet out of his wallet.

Boldly she took the condom and put it on, not as easy a feat as she'd have imagined. By the time she was done, he was trembling and she couldn't get him inside her fast enough.

"No," he said when she tried to pull him onto the desk with her. "It won't hold us."

The desk was old and rickety, and making loud, creaking, protesting noises, but with Mike stroking her halfway back to bliss, she couldn't think. He craned his neck and looked toward the shelving unit, making her laugh breathlessly. "Not the shelves."

Scooping her up, he started toward them anyway, and she wasn't so far gone that she couldn't imagine them collapsing to the floor in a loud heap that would bring the custodian running. "Mike, no."

He turned abruptly, and before she could say another word, he had her against the office door. She'd barely spread her thighs when he buried himself deeply inside her. At the feel of him filling her beyond full, her eyes fluttered closed, her heart raged. Her senses soared. *"Yes."*

Another powerful stroke pounded both her

and the door, and she cried out again, completely lost, as always with him. She might have been terrified, even furious, at his mastery over her, but if his hoarse groan and quivering limbs were any indication, he was just as lost as she.

And then he lifted his head, his eyes dark with passion, need and a hunger so fierce it took her breath. Holding her gaze captive within his, he started to take them both right over the edge. "Look at me," he all but growled.

"I am. Mike, I am."

"Don't stop. Don't ever stop seeing me, even after—" He broke off when she tossed her head back and arched against him, already shuddering with another orgasm.

He followed.

They were still damp and trembling, and still quite breathless, when the knock came at the door.

"Corrine?" It was Stephen, and he sounded worried.

And wary.

"We heard some banging," he called out. "Just wanted to make sure you were okay. Corrine?"

Horrified, stunned and still wrapped around Mike as if she'd been trying to climb his body—

which of course she had!—she went utterly still, staring at Mike. Mike, who'd promised her they were alone.

"Corrine? Is that Mike in there with you?"

"I'll be right with you," she somehow managed to reply.

Which was worse? Being caught in this compromising position, with Mike still buried deep inside her, or the look on his face? A look that didn't hold surprise so much as acceptance. "How did this happen?" she whispered. "My God, Mike, you said they were gone. You didn't do this on purpose, did you?"

He didn't so much as blink, but let go of her thighs so she could slide down his still hard, still hot body.

She stood there, naked and shaking, as fury mounted, along with humiliation. "You did."

Turning away, he reached for his pants, the long, leanly muscled lines of his sleek back drawing her even now. "Is that what you think?" he asked. "That I would? That I could?"

Where were her panties? Oh perfect, they were hanging off the filing cabinet. "I don't know. Why don't you just answer the question?"

He left his pants unfastened as he turned to face her. "Because you should know better."

11

HE FELT GUILTY, no doubt. But not for the reason Corrine seemed to think he should. No matter what she believed, he had not made love to her at work so that they would get caught.

He'd done it because he could no more stop breathing than not take her. That they'd been in her office *should* have been enough to stop him, to bring him to his senses, but that was just another sign of how far gone he was.

He'd taken her, hard, against the door, for crying out loud, and while he was furious at himself, one look at Corrine's dark face told him she was even more furious.

But damn it, she'd had an equal part in this.

In less than sixty seconds, she put herself together, looking like the commander once more. Mike watched, fascinated in spite of himself by the transformation. When she'd smoothed her hair back, straightened her shoulders and was reaching for the door, he whistled low and long. "That's amazing," he said, sounding a little bitter in spite of himself. "How you do that—go from a warm, hot, loving woman to cold, hard and centered, all in the blink of an eye."

It was a direct hit—he knew it had to be—and yet it didn't faze her. She glared daggers at him. "We weren't going to tell anyone."

"News flash. I think it's too late."

"I'm not going to forgive you for this."

He nodded, as if she hadn't just stabbed him right in the heart. "Because you think I did this to you on purpose." That she could even think it made him sick, but before they could have that particular battle, she pulled open the door and faced what he knew was her greatest fear—exposure.

Stephen was standing there, waiting.

"Good news," Corrine said briskly. "We've been working our butts off for months now, and given that we're in stall mode until the arrival of the new equipment, not to mention the computer programming glitch, we're all entitled to take a long weekend." She checked her watch, studied the date, cool as a cucumber, miles from the woman who'd been shuddering in orgasm only moments ago. "It's Thursday now. I don't want to see either of you again until Monday. I'll call the others."

Normally this dictate would be greeted with whoops and hollers, and the backs of quickly retreating astronauts as they hightailed it out of the space center, and maybe even Texas.

But no matter how good Corrine was, she couldn't sidetrack Stephen so easily.

"Damn," he whispered, looking over his shoulder to make sure they were alone. "Do you guys have any idea how noisy you were?"

Corrine blanched, but otherwise showed no outward sign of emotion. "Did you hear what I just said?"

"Yeah, time off, whatever. But—"

"What is it you need?" Corrine asked with that famed chilly voice.

"Need?" Blankly, Stephen looked at them. "Um…"

"Okay, then. See you on Monday." Corrine went to close her office door, then seemed to remember Mike was still standing behind her. Turning, she sent him a get-out-of-here look.

He wasn't going anywhere, damn it, not until they talked this out.

"I need a moment," she said.

He just bet she did. But no matter what she wanted, this moment was not going to go away with a flick of her wrist. Knowing that, he turned to Stephen. "Look, I'm not sure what you heard, but—"

"You don't want to know."

Corrine closed her eyes.

"But if you twist my arm," Stephen said, watching them both with growing amusement as his shock faded, "I heard the banging first." He slapped his hand on the wall with a rhythmic sound that could have come from a set of drums...or two adults having wild, unbridled, out-of-control sex against the door. "Just like that."

"Okay," Corrine said quickly. "Bottom line. I'm human, okay? But it's after hours, and I refuse to apologize for what amounts to my own personal business." She grabbed Mike's elbow and pulled him out of her office.

Then, before he could so much as blink, she went back in and slammed the door, shutting them out.

The lock clicked into place.

Stephen looked at Mike speculatively. "I guess that's that, huh?"

"Yes," Mike said, relieved he wasn't going to press or tease him. "That's that."

"Don't worry. It wasn't really all that obvious, anyway."

"Okay." Mike sighed. "Good."

"I mean, really, you could have been doing anything in there. Copying. Faxing. Computer stuff. Anything."

That's right, Mike told himself. They could have been doing anything, anything at all.

"Except for the 'Don't stop, Mike, oh, please don't stop' part," Stephen said. "That sorta gave you away, big guy."

"Hey, we *could* have been working! She really likes her work!"

Stephen just snorted, then looked at Mike for a long moment.

"What? You have something to say, say it."

"Well, I could tell you how incredibly stupid this is."

"Yeah."

"Or I could ask for details."

Mike frowned. "You're going to make me hurt you, Stephen."

"Oh, boy. Tell me you're not in love, man. Tell me you're not *that* stupid."

"Why would falling in love be stupid?" Mike asked, far too defensively.

"That's not the stupid part. Unless you're falling in love with the Ice Queen."

"Her name is Corrine."

Stephen let out a moan at that. "Oh man. You are. Damn, Mike. You're in deep."

Yeah. *Damn, Mike.*

And then finally he was alone, staring at the shut office door, wondering at the three things that had just happened to him.

One, he'd lost control and made love to Corrine at work, putting them in an incredibly compromising position.

Two, she was never going to forgive him for it.

And three, he'd just realized Stephen might have stumbled onto something, in which case Mike was in a far bigger mess than even he could get out of. Fact was, he still wanted her, and there was nothing physical about it.

That's not the stupid part. Unless you're falling in love with the Ice Queen.

Which he was. Lord, wouldn't his brothers get a kick out of this? He, the man who was afraid of nothing except for maybe commitment, now suddenly wanted with all his heart to be committed to a woman who was not only his commander, but who didn't believe in any weakness. And he was certain she would consider this need of his a biggie.

He wanted a commitment, with Corrine.

Mike actually staggered at that, and wished for a chair. There wasn't one, so he sank to the floor and stared at her still-closed office door.

What was happening to him? To his satisfyingly single, devil-may-care, wild existence?

He wished he knew. Ah, hell, forget that. He did know. He knew exactly.

CORRINE PACED HER OFFICE but no matter how long she walked, the images wouldn't go away. Her, with her back to the wall, legs shrink-wrapped around Mike, head thrown back as she let him take her hard and fast.

Let him take her.

She'd never *let* anyone take her in her entire life. No, she'd demanded it, and the memory of that now burned.

And everyone knew.

Well, whatever. It was done and she was not

going to sit around and cry over spilled milk. So her team knew. She'd deal with that. What she couldn't deal with was having it happen again. Ever.

Grabbing the phone, she pounded out a number. "Mom," she said with relief when her mother picked up. "I miss you." An understatement. Nowhere on earth did she ever feel so good, so comfortable, so happy in her own skin, as she did with her family. "I have three days off, and I'm coming home."

When she'd dealt with her mother's joy, she picked up her purse, ignored her briefcase and hauled open her office door.

Tripping over Mike, she fell right into his lap.

His arms came around her and, wrapped in his warm strength, she forgot to hate him.

"You okay?" he murmured, and that voice, God, that sexy voice, reminded her.

Scrambling to her knees, she pointed at him. *"You."*

He was sitting crosslegged, right there on the floor, looking, to her satisfaction, every bit as miserable as she'd felt before she'd called home. "Me," he agreed.

"Why are you sitting on the floor?"

"I'm not sure you'd believe it. I don't hardly believe it myself," he muttered. "And anyway, it occurred to me, leaving you this mad might be a really bad idea."

With as much dignity as she could, she stood, then sent him a withering glance when he reached out and stopped her from leaving. "Now's not a good time to take me on, Mike."

"I realize that." He held her anyway. "I want you to look me in the eyes, Corrine, and tell me you really believe I did this to hurt you. That I took you against the door of your office for the sole purpose of letting everyone around us know what's going on."

Of course she couldn't look him in the eyes and tell him that. "Now is a bad time."

"Look at me, damn it—" He grappled with her when she fought him. "Tell me."

He was fierce and hurt and full of bad temper. Well, so was she, so she shrugged him off and reached for the purse she'd dropped. "Goodbye, Mike."

She headed for the bathroom to clean up. When she came out he was still there, waiting. Not acknowledging him she turned to leave.

She was halfway down the hall before she realized he was right behind her. Silent. Brooding. She ignored him all the way to her car, even though she wanted to grab him, wanted to hold on to him, lay her head on his shoulder and forget the rest of the world existed.

What a weakness. It terrified her. "Don't even think about following me." She got in her car, started it and pictured the next three days of peace and quiet.

No Mike.

And in the not-too-distant future, after their mission was complete, he'd be out of her life for more than just three days. He'd be gone for good.

Things would be great, she'd be fine and her life would get back to normal. But the truth was, she wasn't fine and nothing would ever be normal again. Not without Mike.

Starting the car, she looked straight ahead and resisted putting her head on the steering wheel to have a good, and very rare, pity party. Mike would be watching, she knew.

IN HIS DUMBEST MOVE since decorating his high-school math teacher's house with toilet paper after a particularly rough test, Mike followed Corrine.

Not that he easily kept up with her on the freeway; the woman was a holy terror, dodging through traffic left and right, making him wince.

She wasn't going to her condo.

It took less than thirty minutes to arrive in a lovely, quiet little suburb where there were white picket fences and pretty yards with flowers and SUVs and children playing—a world away from the military childhood he'd had.

Having spent the past ten years in Russia, in the teeming, overcrowded cities there, he was experiencing quite a culture shock.

Corrine got out of her car, ran up the walk of one exceptionally pretty house and embraced an older couple. There was a beaming smile across her usually solemn face.

And he understood.

She'd come home. Interesting, as he'd never thought of her as the family type. But then again, he'd never thought he'd find himself chasing down a woman he couldn't get out of his head.

Well, meeting her family ought to do it, really. That should bring on both hives *and* the need to run far and fast.

He was counting on it, anyway.

He parked and got out, not sure of his next

move, or even what he really wanted. Maybe for Corrine to acknowledge she'd been unfair to him back there in her office. Or maybe for her to tell him what the hell they had, because he'd feel better if he could somehow label this whole thing.

He knew the exact moment she sensed him; she stiffened and turned, then frowned. He imagined she growled as well, but he was, thankfully, far enough away that he could only hear the birds chirping and the light breeze rustling the trees in the yard.

Oh, and his own nerves. He could hear those loud and clear.

A glutton for punishment, he moved closer.

"From work," she muttered over her shoulder, obviously in response to her mother's question. "He's my pilot. No, don't look at him, maybe he'll go away."

"Corrine Anne!" Her mother looked shocked and horrified. "That is no way to greet a guest!"

Now Corrine looked directly into Mike's eyes, her own gaze filled with dread, resignation. Fear. Everything he was feeling.

There! he thought. *We're in this together, baby.*

"Hello," said the man who he assumed was

Corrine's father. He thrust out his hand. "Donald Atkinson."

"*Dr.* Donald Atkinson," Corrine corrected. "My father." She gestured to the petite, dark-haired woman next to her, who was watching Mike closely, brimming with curiosity. "And this is my mother. Dr. Louisa Atkinson." She smiled sweetly. "And now you can go."

This was going to require finesse. "We need to talk, Corrine."

"Actually, Mike, we don't."

"I know you're mad at me, but—"

"Not here. I'm…busy. Really busy."

"Why do you keep running?"

"*Running?*" She nearly gaped, then seemed to remember their audience and slammed her mouth shut. "I never run. Now go away, Mike."

"Of course he can't go away, darling," her mother said, stepping forward and reaching out a hand to Mike. "He hasn't even come inside yet."

He took her hand immediately, expecting a handshake, but found himself pulled into her warm arms for a welcoming hug. "Well," he said, at an utter loss. Held tight in her embrace, he finally settled for patting her back uncertainly. "Uh…nice to meet you, Dr. Atkinson."

"Oh, just Louisa."

"Mom." Corrine didn't look like a commander at the moment, nor the lover who'd rocked his world; she looked like a peeved daughter. "He doesn't belong here."

Louisa shot her daughter a long look. "I raised you better than that." She smiled at Mike. "We don't stand on formality here. Come in." She slipped an arm through his and led him toward the front door. "So you work with my daughter? All the things you people are doing up there in space, it just blows my mind. Did you get the solar panels to work properly? And what about that complicated computer communications system? What a shame, the troubles, this close to launch. Well, let's not think about that now, hmm? Donald, honey, get the door, will you? And Corrine, put on a pot of water, please. Now, Mike." She squeezed his hand. "Tell me all about yourself. Where are you from? I find that all of you astronauts have such fascinating backgrounds. Corrine's included," she said with a delighted little laugh.

Somehow Mike found himself up the steps, through the front door and sitting in a charming, warm, open living room with a cup of hot tea in his hands.

Corrine paced the length of the room, pausing every five seconds or so to give him a glare that he would have sworn amused her mother all the more.

It should have been awkward, showing up here unannounced and uninvited, but it felt right. And as he opened up for the first time in a long time, he decided Corrine was just going to have to get used to it.

"Oh my goodness," Louisa said, shaking her head after he'd told her a little about himself. "All those years in Russia. What a wonderful experience! I went there for a conference, several years ago now, and I found it to be one of the most beautiful yet haunting places on earth. How lucky you are, to receive that heritage from your mother."

And just that simply, Mike fell in love. He couldn't help it; he had no defenses against a mother, any mother. His had been gone for so long, and his world had always been lacking in any maternal presence or influence whatsoever. But Louisa crossed all barriers and entered his heart.

He looked up and caught Corrine's eye. She'd gone still, and now she was looking at him with something new, something he couldn't place. "What?" he asked softly, but she only shook her head.

And yet her irritation at having him there seemed to diminish. When her parents left the room, ostensibly for cookies, Mike knew it was to give them some privacy.

"You like them," Corrine said with a sigh. "I couldn't have imagined you here, holding a teacup, making nice. But here you are."

"I couldn't have imagined you here, either. But here you are."

"And here *we* are."

"Yeah." He reached out and touched her hand, wanting, needing, yearning for so much it hurt, and yet he didn't have the words. "What now, Corrine?"

"That depends."

"On?"

"On why you're here. Why are you really here, Mike?"

He opened his mouth, but as he didn't have a clear answer for that, or at least one he understood enough to explain, he closed it again.

Looking oddly deflated, she pulled back.

"What did you want me to say?" he asked in turn.

"That's just it," she whispered with a heart-breaking sigh. "I don't know, either."

12

NO DOUBT ABOUT IT, Mike's presence in her family home scared Corrine, really scared her.

He looked good here, comfortable. Confused, she took a walk. Unsatisfied, she ended up in her parents' garden, where she found her father showing off his prize roses to Mike.

Both of them were hunkered down in the dirt, their backs to her, admiring the growth of a flower.

It was a contradiction in terms, these so very masculine men surrounded by such sweet, feminine beauty, and yet that was one of the things she loved so much about her dad.

He didn't fit into a type. She stood there, rooted by a sudden realization.

That was why she liked Mike as well.

Oh, God, it was true. He was an astronaut, which meant by definition he should have been cocky, arrogant and in possession of a certain recklessness. A wild adventurer.

He *was* those things, but he was also so much more. And watching as he reached out now and touched the tip of a blooming rose with such joy, with his entire face lit up, made her heart tighten.

The reason for being one half of a couple had always escaped Corrine, mostly because she'd never wanted to be half of anything. She'd certainly never wanted anyone able to veto her decisions, or God forbid, make them for her.

And yet her parents were a couple, a solid one, and for years they'd managed to work things out with an ease that Corrine always admired but never understood. They were both well-educated overachievers, stubborn as hell, and single-minded, so really, their success was one big mystery.

A mystery Corrine suddenly, urgently needed to solve.

SHE WAITED UNTIL dinner time, when she found both her parents together in the kitchen. Her father was chopping vegetables. Her mother was standing over him, shaking her head. "You're not cutting diagonally, dear. You need to—"

"I think I know how to cut a tomato, Louisa."

"No, obviously you don't. You have to—"

"Louisa, honey? Either let me be or order take-out."

"Take-out sounds wonderful."

"Don't you dare," Donald said, smiling when his teasing wife laughed at him.

"How do you do that?" Corrine asked, baffled by the mix of temper and affection. "How do you fight over a tomato and still love each other?"

"Forty years of practice." Her father grinned. "You going to marry Mike and learn how?"

"No!"

Louisa sighed. "Well, darn."

"Mom, I didn't invite him here."

"But he followed you." Her mother sent her a dreamy look. "He loves you, you know."

"*What?*"

"He's head over heels. Ga-ga. Fallen off the cliff."

Corrine felt the color drain from her face, but managed a perfectly good laugh. "You've been dipping into the cooking sherry."

"No, really. He—" At the elbow in her ribs, Louisa glared at her husband, who gave her a wordless glance. Whatever unspoken communication they'd shared, Louisa went quiet on the matter. But she did manage to get the knife from him and push him toward the door.

"I can tell when I'm not wanted," he said, kissing his wife on the cheek before he went.

"Why did you argue with him over the knife, Mom? He was just trying to help."

"Oh, I know."

"But you kicked him out."

"Kicked him out... Oh, honey." Louisa laughed. "You think I hurt his feelings. Trust me, I didn't. It's just that he always cooks, and he's worked an eighty-hour week already. The poor man is dead on his feet, but he didn't want to leave me alone to do the work. It's just a little game we play, that's all."

Corrine glanced at the swinging double doors where her father had vanished, and knew the mysteries of cohabiting were still escaping her. "A game."

"Yes." Louisa set down the knife and smiled easily. "Of love."

Mike poked his head in the kitchen. "Can I help?" He moved to the cutting board and picked up the knife Corrine's mother had just set down. "I'm good at slicing veggies," he said, following Louisa's diagonal cuts.

Corrine's mother positively beamed. "What a handy man you are." She shot Corrine a telling look, pointing at Mike's back and mouthing the words, *Loves you.*

Corrine rolled her eyes and turned away, but that lasted no more than a second before she had to crane her neck and stare at him. He was the same person he'd always been: the same dark hair and darker eyes; the same long, leanly muscled body that made her mouth water; the same here-I-am attitude that both drew and annoyed her at the same.

So why was she looking at him in such a different light here in the house where she'd been raised?

"Louisa." Donald stuck his head back in the kitchen and waved a checkbook. "Babe, this thing is a mess. I can't figure out how much money is in here."

"Look at the bottom line, hon," Louisa said, pulling more salad makings out of the fridge.

"Which bottom line? You have three of them here."

"Oh." Louisa straightened, lettuce in one hand, a beet in the other. "Well, the first is in case the check I lost clears the bank. If I lost it *before* I wrote it, which is entirely likely, then that wouldn't be necessary. Hence the second number."

Donald sighed. "And the third?"

"Why, that's what we'll have when my automatic deposit comes in tomorrow."

"Tomorrow."

"That's right."

"But what do we have *today*?"

"I just told you, it's either—"

"Never mind!" He withdrew his head and vanished.

Louisa grinned. "Perfect."

"Why is annoying him to distraction perfect?" Corrine asked, confused beyond belief.

"I just bought his birthday present." Louisa grinned. "And if he wasn't so annoyed, he'd have found the check entry. He would talk me into giving him that present early, no doubt about it. Now he'll toss the checkbook aside and give up." She laughed. "Secret kept."

"Louisa!" Donald bellowed from the other room. "I'm going out to chop wood!"

"Good Lord," Louisa murmured. "I meant to have that nice young man down the street do that before your father tried it himself. Last year he nearly lost his fingers."

Mike set down the knife. "I'll go help him."

"Bless you," Corrine's mother said fervently, giving him a quick hug.

Corrine watched pleasure dance across Mike's face as he hugged her back, far more easily this time.

Why was he still here, damn him?

"He's a wonderful man," her mother said when he was gone. "Shame on you for keeping your feelings to yourself."

Out the kitchen window Mike reappeared, walking toward her father.

Corrine forced herself to turn away. "He's a pest."

Louisa laughed. "Okay, hon. If that's how you want to play this thing. Just tell me he's not an adventurous, intelligent, gorgeous man and I'll believe you."

"I hadn't noticed."

"Uh-huh."

"Okay, he's adventurous."

"And intelligent."

"Yes."

"And gorgeous."

"Mom, please."

"And gorgeous," Louisa repeated.

"Okay, fine." Corrine sighed. "And gorgeous."

"He's a keeper, Corrine."

A keeper. Her heart tugged. "Yeah, about that. Keepers. I don't understand something." She drew a deep breath. "You and Dad. What keeps you together? You should have killed each other by now."

"Why? Because we're two strong-minded, strong-willed people?"

"Well...yeah."

"That doesn't mean we can't make peace over such simple things as making dinner and paying the bills."

"It just seems..." Corrine once again glanced out the window. Watched Mike's muscles bunch and flex as he raised the ax over his head and brought it down, perfectly splitting a log in two.

Every hormone in her body reacted, but that was physical. Would she still want in him in forty years? "Hard," she said, no pun intended. "It seems hard."

Louisa looked shocked and more than a little annoyed. "I can't believe we didn't show you better than that, after all these years."

"You're telling me this is easy?"

"Of course not! But it's beautiful anyway, and worth all the work."

"You work at it?" she asked doubtfully. What she'd seen so far didn't seem like work so much as...good luck.

"Goodness, darling." Louisa let out a little laugh. "I think I'm insulted that you have to ask. Yes, we work hard. You can't believe such a loving relationship comes naturally."

"It does in the romance novels," Corrine muttered, taking another quick peek at Mike. He straightened and pulled off his shirt, tossing it aside before once again lifting the ax.

Oh. My. God.

Muscles. Skin shining with sweat. She purposely looked away. And this time, she wasn't going to take another sneak peek!

"Phooey," Louisa was saying. "Nothing this good comes easy. It takes compromise." She picked up the paring knife again. "Give and take. And after so many years, it just keeps getting better and better."

"It does?" What was this silly hope that sprang through Corrine at that? What did it matter if marriage was wonderful? She wasn't planning on trying.

Was she?

Oh God. She was. She was planning on exactly that. Putting a hand to her suddenly damp forehead, she sank to a chair.

"Corrine? Corrine, honey, what's the matter?" Her mother dropped the paring knife and rushed over. "You look terribly pale."

"Oh, Mom. It's…it's…"

"What? It's what?" She knelt down and gripped Corrine's knees. "Are you going to be sick? Do you need a bucket?"

"Yes, I think I do." Corrine gulped, but then managed a hysterical laugh when her mother turned to leave. Grabbing Louisa's wrist, she shook her head. "No, it's not that kind of sickness. It's my heart, you see." And she rubbed the ache that had settled there the day she'd met Mike and had never, not once in all these months, gone away.

"Oh, dear Lord. You've got heart problems? You didn't tell me! We'll get a second opinion. Your father—"

"Mom, it's…" She took a big gulp of air. "It's love. I think I'm in love with Mike. I just realized it, just now, and it's making me sick."

"Oh, darling!"

"Don't look so excited," Corrine warned, pointing a finger at the joy scrambling across her mother's face. "This is a terrible thing. I actually—" she pressed both hands to her heart now "—I actually want forever with him."

Louisa's eyes filled. "Oh, baby."

"Don't you dare cry."

Louisa sniffed and wiped a tear from her cheek. "I'm not." Then a sob escaped and she slapped a hand over her mouth. "Really, I'm not."

"Mom!"

"I can't help it," Louisa cried. "It's just that I'm so thrilled for me. He's just what I always wanted in a son-in-law."

"No! Mike can't know!"

"What? Why not?"

"Don't you see? This can't happen. It just can't. It's an impossible situation, for a million different reasons." Though all of them were crowding her head, she couldn't put words to any of them.

"Name one," her mother commanded.

"There's…well…"

Louisa cocked a brow. "Why, Corrine?"

"Yes," Mike said from the doorway, with a perfectly indescribable look on his face. "Why?"

Corrine's stomach dropped to her toes. So did her heart, and all her other vital organs.

How much had he heard?

There was no telling from the look on his face. "I—I thought you were chopping wood."

"I was. Until I got the strange feeling there was something far more interesting going on in here." He leaned back against the doorjamb, casual as you please. "I was right."

"Yes, well." Corrine leaped to her feet and became a whirlwind of activity, busying herself by straightening up an already tidy kitchen. "We were just—"

"Talking about me," he said, taking her shoulders, turning her to face him.

How had he moved so fast? Reluctantly she looked into those dark eyes, thinking *Please don't have heard me, oh please don't have heard.*

But those eyes were filled with knowing, and she swallowed hard. "You caught it all, didn't you?" she whispered.

"Every word."

13

SHE LOVED HIM.

Mike hadn't imagined it, had never dared give thought to the possibility. But now his heart was racing, his entire body humming. He could think of nothing else. "Say it again," he demanded.

"I don't think so."

"Please?"

That surprised her, and he realized he hadn't often shown her his polite, gentle, tender side, not unless they were in bed.

That would change, because he intended to make her the happiest woman on earth.

"I think you should go," she said calmly, her eyes alone showing her panic.

"Nope, that wasn't what you said." He cocked his head and smiled, though he was so nervous he could hardly draw a breath. "Try again."

"No, I mean I think you should leave. Now."

He looked at Louisa, who gave a sympathetic

shrug. "You have things to discuss," she said. "I'm going to give you some privacy."

"We don't need it," Corrine said quickly, but her mother only put a finger to her lips.

"Listen to him, honey. For once, slow down and listen."

Louisa left, and Corrine stood there looking cornered. When cornered, Mike knew, she came out fighting.

But fight or discuss, calm or agitated, they were doing this. "We can make it," he said softly. "We can make this work, no matter what our jobs are, no matter how different we are, no matter what. Are you getting this?" She studied her shoes. "If we try hard enough, nothing can stop us," he insisted.

"I can think of lots of things to stop us."

"Such as?" He smiled in the face of her fear, even as his heart constricted. "I know it's terrifying." Close enough to touch now, he took her hands in his. "Truth is, I've been terrified since the day I met you, and I didn't realize why until just a moment ago, when I heard you say you love me."

She made a sound of misery and fury, and tried to tug her hands free.

He held on.

She tugged again, but he was quicker and

stronger. "I love you back, Corrine. I always have and I always will."

She hadn't so much as blinked. "What did you say?"

"I said I love you back." He waited while that sank in, while her eyes went from heated to glassy with shock. "I want this to work."

"Work."

"Between us. And I want forever. As in the white dress, the minivan, kids..."

"Kids."

"Or not." He shrugged. "I can go either way, unless we're talking about us. Because that's one thing I'm pretty set on, Corrine. *You.*"

"You're set."

He had to smile. "You're sounding like a parrot. Tell me this is good news. Tell me you meant what you said to your mom. That you know we can do this."

She only stared at him.

"Tell me something. *Anything.*"

"You love me."

"Yes."

"You want to get married."

"Yes. Wait, I didn't do that right at all." He dropped to one knee, then reached for her hand.

"Corrine." His heart was in his throat. "You waltzed into my life and changed it forever with your incredible smile and fierce passion. You—"

"My, God. Are you...*proposing*?"

"I'm trying."

"You'd better hurry, then." A half laugh escaped her. "I don't think my legs are going to hold me."

"Did I mention your bossy ways?"

"Mike—"

"Yes," he said with a laugh, even as his throat burned. "I'm proposing. I love you, Corrine. I want to love you forever. Will you marry me?"

"If it's just passion and a smile you're attached to, I give those to you freely. You don't have to marry me for them."

"I know." He tugged her down to her knees in front of him. "But I *want* to marry you."

"I'm still ranked higher at work," she warned.

He had to laugh again. "This is not a trick. I actually *want* to wake up next to you every morning for the rest of my life."

"You've seen me first thing in the morning, right?" she asked with suspicion.

"No, actually I haven't."

"This is not a joke."

"Nope, it's not. The answer is yes or no."

"How can it be that easy?" she cried. "My God, you're looking at me with a straight face proposing m-m—"

"Marriage. The word is *marriage*."

"We have no business doing this."

He cupped her face, waited until her wild eyes settled on his. "Do you love me?"

"This is ridiculous."

"Do you?"

Her hands came up to cover his. "Yes," she said simply. "It's crazy, but I do. I love you, Mike."

"Then everything else is a piece of cake," he said, the fist around his heart loosening for the first time since he'd met her. He could have flown to Mars without a spacecraft. "Be my commander, be my lover, my best friend, my spouse. Be my life, Corrine."

"For better, for worse, and maybe lots of worse?"

"Bring it on. All of it. Marry me."

"I will, Mike. Yes, I will."

_____Epilogue_____

One Year Later

"THE SPACE SHUTTLE LANDED without a hitch today," the television anchor announced. "Thanks to the hard and amazing work of a select few, we're one step closer to completing the International Space Station."

Corrine sighed with pleasure, both because the mission had been successful, and because her husband had come up behind her, slipped his big hands around her and was rubbing her stomach.

"Nice?" he murmured, dipping down to kiss her neck.

"Any nicer and you'll send me into labor." His hands stroked her nine-month-pregnant belly until she wanted to melt with bliss. "Just saw the news," she told him. "They're back. The landing was perfect."

"Not as perfect as ours last year."

"I know." She sighed again, remembering just

how wonderfully successful their own mission had been. "I'm ready to go back up."

Mike laughed and turned her in his arms. "Can you wait until you give birth, do you think?"

"What do you think he'll be when he grows up?" she wondered, feeling the baby within her kick with the velocity of a rocket.

"*She'll* be anything she wants, though I imagine stubborn as hell, poor baby. Just like her mommy."

"I'm not stubborn."

"Uh-huh. And I'm not the luckiest man on the planet."

"You're the luckiest man on the planet?"

He smiled that just-for-her smile he had, the one that made her feel like the most special, precious woman alive. Even after all this time, her heart went pitter-patter. Her mother had been right, as always. Love was worth the work.

"What?" he asked with a little smile, his thumb gliding over her lower lip, his eyes full of so much warmth and love her throat tightened.

Her stomach contracted.

It wasn't the first contraction, or the second, and she knew the time had come. "I love you, Mike."

"You say that as though you just realized it," he said with a little laugh.

"No." She hid her wince as the contraction stole her breath. "I've always known," she managed to say, watching his eyes mist. "Oh, and Mike?" Unable to keep it in, she gasped as the contraction ended. "It's time."

"Baby, we can't. You're too far along for love-making now."

"No, I mean it's *time*."

He blinked, then his jaw dropped. "Oh my God."

The look of pure terror on his face made her laugh in spite of her pain. "You've flown every aircraft known to man. You've traveled off this planet. And yet the thought of having a baby terrifies you?"

He scooped her up into his arms. "Sit down," he demanded.

"I already am," she said, as he paced the room with her.

"We need to get organized!"

"We are." She pointed to the packed bag by their front door.

"We need a doctor!"

"Maybe," she conceded, pulling him down for

a quick kiss. "But honestly, Mike, everything I need, or will need, is right here. He's holding me."

"God, Corrine." He rubbed his cheek to hers. "You've given me everything I could ever need, too."

And five hours later, she gave him even more. A beautiful baby girl with dark, dark eyes and wild hair and a fierce, demanding cry that reminded him of his amazing, accomplished, beautiful wife.

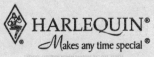

HARLEQUIN®
Temptation.

Look for bed, breakfast and more...!

*Some of your favorite Temptation authors are
checking in early at Cooper's Corner Bed and Breakfast*

In May 2002:

#877 *The Baby and the Bachelor*
Kristine Rolofson

In June 2002:

#881 *Double Exposure*
Vicki Lewis Thompson

In July 2002:

#885 *For the Love of Nick*
Jill Shalvis

In August 2002 things heat up even more at
Cooper's Corner. There's a whole year of intrigue
and excitement to come—twelve fabulous books
bound to capture your heart and mind!

Join all your favorite Harlequin authors
in Cooper's Corner!

HARLEQUIN®
Makes any time special ®

Visit us at www.eHarlequin.com

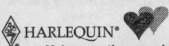